COMING OUT
maria

sylvia aguilar-zéleny

EPIC
Press

Maria
Coming Out: Book #4

Written by Sylvia Aguilar-Zéleny

Copyright © 2016 by Abdo Consulting Group, Inc.

Published by EPIC Press™
PO Box 398166
Minneapolis, MN 55439

All rights reserved.

Printed in the United States of America.

Cover design by Nicole Ramsay
Images for cover art obtained from Shutterstock.com
Edited by Nancy Cortelyou

LIBRARY OF CONGRESS CATALOGING-IN-PUBLICATION DATA

Aguilar-Zéleny, Sylvia.
Maria / Sylvia Aguilar-Zéleny.
p. cm. — (Coming out)
Summary: After relocating to East L.A., Maria rediscovers her familial roots and
becomes empowered like never before. She can't continue hiding that she is a lesbian
when she meets Natalia, the one person who will turn Maria's life upside down.
ISBN 978-1-68076-010-1 (hardcover)
1. Homosexuality—Fiction. 2. Lesbians—Fiction. 3. Lesbian teenagers—Fiction.
4. Coming out (Sexual orientation)—Fiction. 5. Young adult fiction. I. Title.
[Fic]—dc23
2015932732

*To my loving mother, a beautiful woman
who taught me that love is love*

CHAPTER ONE
hands off

MASTURBATING. MASTURBATION. MASTURBATOR. Sister Helen writes those three words on the board. We all look at each other. I hear my classmates giggling. A few of them, girls who started shaving in elementary school and who have already made out with a boy or two, make a face as if those were the most boring words in the world. Sister Helen tells us these three words are equal to sin. "A sin of the body," she says, "and that is the worst kind."

She tries to conclude her lesson when one of the more experienced girls says, "Isn't killing, or taking the name of the Lord in vain, way worse than touching yourself, Sister?"

The whole class goes quiet and stares at Sister Helen and her big, grey mustache and her bad temper.

All Sister Helen says is, "Class dismissed."

"Masturbating. Masturbation. Masturbator." It wasn't the first time I had heard those "concepts" because I knew them, I knew them well. Yes, I was a masturbator. Big time.

It all started about four years ago, when my sister got sick and was in and out of the hospital. I spent a lot of time alone and discovered the real pleasure of taking a bath. I liked leaving the faucet running in the bathtub—not full force—just hard enough. Then, I would lie back in the warm water and scoot all the way up to the faucet so that the stream would hit me right *there*. I would move my pelvis around and let the water go different places. It felt wonderful, a delicious tingling. I became the cleanest girl in the world. Until Mom caught me doing *it*.

She yelled, "Mari, what on earth are you doing?!" She turned off the faucet, handed me a towel and made me get out. I was not supposed to do that, she said.

"Why?" I asked. "I like it. It, it makes me happy."

Mom replied, "But it's bad, don't do it. You'll get hurt." I didn't argue. You don't argue with Mom unless you like losing.

Baths were pretty much off limits for me. "A quick shower and then off to bed," Mom would say. If I did convince my mom to let me take a bath, she would find excuses to come in the bathroom like a dozen times.

Soon after being caught I discovered that moving my index finger, up and down, or rubbing and rubbing and rubbing and rubbing myself down there with the palm of my hand would do the trick too. It felt great.

This was back when Glo and I shared the room.

I don't know if she ever heard me or saw me doing something. I wonder if she ever did it too? That seems impossible, though. Glo was always tired, always in pain, always sick. Then, as she got sicker and sicker, I started losing the pleasure of doing *it*.

Truth is, life went from bad to worse for my family. Not long after Glo died, Dad told us that the company he worked for was going bankrupt thanks to a lawsuit. Mom did not have a job. She had quit when Glo's health got worse. Believe me, touching myself really hadn't been on my mind. Until today—thank you, Sister Helen. Now, I only want classes to be over for the day so I can go home to do it.

Doing *it*, I bet, will take my mind off everything. Doing *it*, will make me forget the fact that in a few months, classes will be over and we will start packing to leave Santa Barbara for good. We'll be living in Grandma Sarita's house. East LA, here we come.

* * *

The Immaculate Heart of Mary School used to be a convent. Immaculate, as we call it, is a weird building with labyrinth-like halls. You have to rush to make it from one class to the other before the bell rings, and rushing means bumping into people. I run into the soccer coach, Mrs. Peters. "Hey, Mari, how are you?" she says.

I shrug and smile, "Okay, I guess."

Mrs. Peters takes me by the shoulders and says, "You know I'm here for you, don't you? I've missed you. The whole team misses you. I really hope you will consider coming back to the team."

I don't know what to say other than, "Thank you, Mrs. Peters." She pats me on the back and then points at her watch, "Don't be late for class."

It's been almost a semester since I left the soccer team. I miss it. I miss my teammates and I miss Mrs. Peters, too, but I don't know. I was doing a lousy job. I wasn't focused, and it was affecting everyone.

Gloria was always sick and weak from anemia. At

first, it wasn't a big deal, but then it became serious. She was only sixteen when she was diagnosed with leukemia, and she died just one year later. At first Glo was scared, like she didn't want to die. She wanted to keep going to school, she wanted us all to have normal lives, but that was impossible.

"You are late, Miss Herrera," says Sister Georgette, our math teacher, as I walk in.

"I'm sorry. I ran into Mrs. Peters and . . . " I reply. Sister Georgette puts her index finger to her lips and then points to my chair. She hates me; she hates all of us. Sister Georgette is the kind of nun that would make for a great villain in children's stories. I take my seat and check what my classmates are doing. They all have their textbooks open to chapter seven. Freaking algebra.

"Let's start with problems one, two, and three. In groups of three, start working on these and then we will review them together." I turn around to find partners, but all the smart girls are already taken.

"Wanna work with Paulette and me, Mari?"

"Yeah, like she has any other choice. Look around, Dana, everyone's gone with the nerds."

Paulette and Dana: the James twins. No one likes them all that much, but I do. I think they're funny. They're different from everyone else here. They are blunt and honest. They don't pretend.

I move my chair next to them and start working on the horrible math problems.

"Is it true you're leaving?" Paulette asks.

"Yeah. This will be my last semester here. We're moving away this summer. Now let's . . . " I point to the textbook, trying to make the twins work instead of talk.

I go back to my notebook and pull out my calculator and bang numbers away until Paulette says, "So . . . "

And Dana finishes, "Where are you going?" I pretend not to hear them, but Dana insists, "Maria Herrera, we are talking to you. Where are you going?"

I put down my calculator, take a deep breath, and go, "Number one, don't call me Maria, you know I hate it. Number two, we are moving to Los Angeles. My dad got a job there."

I lied. Of course, I lied. I wasn't gonna to tell them we are moving to East LA, the place my mother and my father were born and raised. I can say Los Angeles, but not East LA; anyway, East LA is in Los Angeles after all, so technically I'm not lying.

"*Los Angeles?*" Paulette gasps.

Sister Georgette turns to us and says, "Are you girls working or having fun?"

"Sorry, Sister."

We work for a few minutes while Sister Georgette hovers nearby, but as soon as she goes to the other side of the classroom, Dana whispers, "You're going to Los Angeles?" Dana's and Paulette's big blue eyes stare at me.

"Yes, I'll finish high school there, and then, who knows?"

"OMG, you have to keep in touch with us, Mari," says Paulette.

"Yes, and you have to invite us sometime," adds

Dana. "The only time our mother took us to LA we just did like a boring kids' tour, and didn't even get to see Melrose Place and Hollywood and . . . "

I smile and say, "Of course, definitely." I have no intention of inviting them. What would the twins say of our house in an East LA *barrio*?

"Aaaaaaand, you must invite us to your Sweet Sixteen. You're coming to ours, aren't you?" Dana asks.

"Our cousins are *very* handsome," Paulette says, "I am sure you'll fall in love with one of them. And, we also have very *pretty* cousins." Why would she say that? I feel tempted to ask, but instead I keep doing my work.

"When is your birthday again?"

I tell them it's in August and that I am not planning to have a Sweet Sixteen, which makes them more interested in talking than in algebra.

"You're not having—" starts Paulette.

"—a Sweet Sixteen party?" continues Dana. Then both of them ask, "Are you serious?"

I put my pencil to my lips and tell them to shut up. Sister Georgette is walking around the classroom. I try to focus and finish solving this problem, but I really, really suck at algebra. Dealing with math was way easier when Glo was around. She would help me at home. See, Glo was great with numbers, physics, and chemistry. She used to say she liked the challenge and the fact that there was only one right answer for everything. During her last weeks, she would review her textbooks. Just like everyone in her class, she was getting ready for the SATs. I guess a part of her believed she still had time, that she was still going to make it.

I'm best at the humanities. Give me English, Journalism, Communications, or Creative Writing and I kick ass. Give me numbers and I rot.

The bell rings and Sister Georgette tells us to work on problems four to eight at home and turn them in by Wednesday. That already sounds like a problem to me. As I am leaving, Dana runs after me and asks if I want to do the homework with them.

"Come on, Mari. We promise no gossip, only numbers. Tomorrow at our place?"

"Well, maybe a little gossip, and some numbers," Paulette says. "I know this gross story about a junior girl who was caught touching herself by one of the sisters."

Dana and I are in shock. She pushes her sister and says, "Get out of here, are you serious?"

Paulette says, "Yes, very serious."

I haven't been friends with the twins all that long. We just started hanging out a few months ago when my best friend Aimée left and I quit the soccer team. The twins make me think of Glo. She was almost two years older than me, but we were very close.

"Okay, I'll be at your place around five tomorrow. Sound good?"

* * *

Mom is on the phone, using her professional voice.

She writes something down, then hangs up and says, "I have an interview at a health services company in LA. If all goes well, I will be working soon."

My mom used to work as a manager at the Santa Barbara Hospital. She has worked in hospitals and clinics her whole life. She's always dreamt about becoming a doctor, but hospital manager is as far as she got. Mom would have made a great doctor, but her father would not let her go to medical school. Who knows why? She was lucky though, she did get to go to community college, unlike her sister, my Aunt Angela, who has been a housewife since she was twenty. Aunt Angela, my mom's only sister, lives in East LA, too.

My mom's side of the family is kinda weird. Mom's father, Grandpa Elias, was born in Mexico. He came to the States when he was a boy, but it seems that he brought the *machista* mentality with him. His wife, Grandma Jane, was American and was raised on a farm somewhere in Oregon. I guess she either didn't see the point of having her daughters go to college, or she didn't want to go against Grandpa Elias' wishes.

"Wow, that sounds great," I tell her, "but how are you scheduling interviews already? Didn't you and Dad say we wouldn't move until the summer?" I open the fridge and take out yesterday's leftover lasagna.

"Well, yes, but it's best to get started now." Mom takes the lasagna out of my hands and puts it back in the fridge. She points at the soup on the stove.

"What if you get hired before June? Will you go on your own?"

"Of course not, silly. Let me pour you some of this," she says.

"I don't want soup," I protest. "You know I hate soup."

"But it's minestrone—fresh cut vegetables, all for you," she says. Our diet changed dramatically when Glo got sick. Not that we had bad habits or anything, it's just that we lived on frozen food for such a long time, you know, because both Mom and Dad worked a lot.

"Fine," I say, "but can I also have a bit of lasagna? Dad was so happy I liked it. He'll be glad I ate it all." Dad's been cooking a lot lately. It's his way of handling stress.

"Can you call Dad? He is in . . . "

"His studio, I know."

Uncle Robert, my Aunt Angela's husband, has offered my dad a job at his furniture store, Casa Nueva, in East LA but Dad is still looking for other options. He says family and business should not mix. The truth is, knowing Dad as I do, it's his ego that won't let him take that job. He's probably wondering how he can manage a furniture store when he used to be much more than that. I don't like Uncle Robert. No one in the family really does, not even my aunt, his wife. He would have been the perfect son that Grandpa Elias and Grandma Jane never had. He's so close-minded, so traditional. So boring. I can't understand why Aunt Angela married him. But I guess it was really nice of him to offer help after the whole thing with Dad's job.

Dad was born in the States. He's the only child of Grandma Sarita, who was a single mother. My dad worked his ass off to get where he is, I mean, where he was. I mean . . . well, you know. He was an executive for almost fifteen years. First he worked in the LA offices, and then he was promoted and we all moved here to Santa Barbara. He doesn't say it, but I know he's still upset about everything that has happened in the last four years. He keeps telling us not to worry. But I think he's the one who is worried. He is the one in shock for having to go back to East LA. "We were very happy to move to Santa Barbara. We wanted to raise you and your sister in a friendlier environment. But you gotta do what you gotta do. Going back will save us some money."

I lie and tell him that I am excited and curious about going back, about finding my roots. But I truly hate the idea of moving and of living in a barrio and going to public school. Not because I am a rich snob, not at all, or maybe I am a little bit, but what really worries me is that I know I will be a target because I'll be the new girl. I just know it.

"Dinner is ready," I tell Dad as I open his studio door. Boxes filled with books are on the floor. "What's all this?" I ask him pointing at the boxes.

"Well, we won't need all these books back in LA so I thought about selling them." He looks at me and sees the shock on my face. "Of course, I will only sell what you really don't wanna keep. I know how much you like history and fiction."

"Historical fiction," I correct him. "And yes, I wanna take a look before you get rid of everything."

"DINNER IS REAAAAADY."

This is Mom's new thing, she yells at us every time she can. It's like she likes giving her lungs and throat a workout all the freaking time.

"You should convince her to put you in charge of the kitchen for good," I tell Dad as we leave the studio. "We could be eating some delicious *picadillo* now and not this healthy stuff Mom has been forcing on us."

"Well, convincing your Mom is not easy. We'll be eating fruits, vegetables, and fish forever. No more steak for us."

"When we get to LA and Grandma gives us an overdose of enchiladas, you'll see," I say.

We both walk to the kitchen. The soup is served.

"Hey, I need to go to the twins' house tomorrow. We have a math assignment."

There was a long silence and I watched my dad's face tighten in grief. We all know that Glo used to help me with my math.

Mom and I miss Glo, but Dad is the one who struggles with the idea of her not being here.

Dad, Mom, and I have our places at the table. It's a small white wooden table for four in the middle of our kitchen. We only use the dining room for special occasions. As we all take our spots, Glo's chair stays empty. It's like everything around us reminds us every day that she is not here. Maybe moving will be healthy for us after all.

"How was school today?" Mom says.

For a second I think of what Sister Helen "taught" us today and I choke on Mom's soup. "Same old stuff. We're just reviewing."

"She's going to her friends' house to study. Today, you said?" Dad asks as he adds a ton of Tabasco to his soup. Mom gives him the eye.

"No. Tomorrow."

"Which friends?" she asks.

"Paulette and Dana," I say. "The James twins." Mom makes a face and drops the spoon in her bowl.

"Oh, Mari, you know I don't like them very much. Their mother lets them do anything they want."

"Come on, Mom, it's not like that. It's just that their mother trusts their judgment."

"And I don't trust yours?"

"I didn't say that. Anyway, we're just going to work on algebra."

"She needs help when it comes to math," Dad says.

Mom nods and says, "Fine."

When we finish eating, the three of us put the dishes away and clean the kitchen. Then Dad goes to his studio and Mom goes back to the living room computer to search for jobs online.

Me? I have a date with the warm water from the handheld showerhead.

The next day we get yet another lesson on the sin of masturbation. It's the topic everywhere: all of the girls are talking about it. Some say it *is* a sin, some say that it isn't. The twins say that everything that feels good becomes a sin.

After dinner at home, Dad drives me to Dana and Paulette's.

"Mari, I thought you were never going to get here," says Dana.

"Why? What is it?" I respond as I walk in the room she and Paulette share.

"This one wouldn't tell me a thing about the girl who was found by the nun. And it's been two days."

"What girl?" I ask.

"You know, doing *something* to herself." I then hear Paulette's laugh coming from the bathroom.

Paulette comes out of the bathroom, still zipping up her pants. "She's dying to know, Mari. When it comes to gossip Dana is worse than I am." Paulette moves clothes, pillows, and blankets to make space for herself on one of the beds. "Okay, let me get comfortable, and I'll tell you what I know." The twins' room is a big, fat mess. Finally, she starts, "So, it seems that Sister Theresa found one of the girls from the soccer team taking a very relaxing shower . . ."

"What do you mean by *relaxing*? Explain," Dana says. Paulette stands up and turns on an invisible faucet and pretends to be showering. She does a great performance. She even grabs an invisible soap and starts scrubbing her arms, shoulders. First she scrubs strong and fast, then she starts moving slowly. We know what she is doing. Dana and I start giggling. Then she pushes her head back and her hips forward. Paulette opens her legs, her arms up on the sides. Her right hand moves slowly to her crotch. Up and down, up and down. Dana and I stop giggling; we are both in shock.

I close my eyes for a second and then I see the water running through her legs. I see the steam, my face starts feeling hot as Paulette starts moaning, "Oh, yes, aahhh, yes, mmmhhh." All of a sudden she stops and covers herself. She makes a different voice and puts her hands on her waist and yells, "Hands off, girl." Then she covers herself with her hands and says, "Sister Theresa, what are you . . . ? No, Sister, let me explain. I was just . . . No, no, Sister, believe me, I wasn't . . . " An invisible Sister Theresa has just caught Paulette in the *act*. She then turns off the faucet and covers herself with a pillow and continues apologizing to Sister Theresa. The shame on her face, the shame in her voice. How is she going to convince the nun that she wasn't doing anything wrong?

Paulette then forgets her dramatization and states, "Then Mother Superior calls the girl's parents and the girl gets detention. Can you believe it?"

"Wait, Pau, you haven't told us—who was it? Who was the girl?!" Dana asks.

"Well, that's exactly what Mari is going to tell us," Paulette says. The twins look at me, and I go, "Me? Why? How? I didn't even know any of this. How am I supposed to know who was caught?"

"Easy, you were on the soccer team, weren't you? For how long?" Paulette asks.

"Yes. Since seventh grade, but that doesn't mean . . . "

"I know you don't actually know, but you know all of them, don't you? I bet you know who it *could* be." Excited, Paulette grabs me by the hands.

"Yes, Mari, yes," Dana says. "Think, think. Which of the girls on the team was it? Who? Who?"

"I don't know. Could be anybody. I have no clue." Both twins look at me, disappointed. "I, I'll have to think about it." I'm not lying. I really have no idea who could have done something like that.

"Okay. You think about it," says Dana.

"Now we should get started on algebra," I say, trying to change the subject. They both nod. Dana gets her backpack and sits back on the floor next to her sister, but Paulette doesn't move. I can feel her staring at me.

"Hey, Listen Mari, we . . . we have another question for you," Paulette says.

Dana elbows her sister and says, "No, Paulette, shhh. Not now."

"What is it?" I ask innocently. I imagine they are going to ask me one of the two questions that everybody has been asking me lately: One, how are you holding up since your sister, you know? Or, two, are you going back to the soccer team? But I'm completely wrong.

Paulette, who is bolder than her twin, says, "Is it true about you and that French girl who was here for one semester? What was her name?" Paulette turns to Dana.

"Aimée," she replies.

"Yes, Aimée. Is it true that you and Aimée, you know, you guys made out?"

Without blinking, without thinking I reply, "What are you talking about?" Paulette and Dana look at each other. I must sound convincing because they both shrug. "Who told you that lie? I was friends with Aimée. Actually, we're still friends, we e-mail each other all the time, but that doesn't mean anything." I act offended and, really, this must be working because then Dana says, "Sorry, Mari, sorry, we didn't mean. It's just, you know how the girls in school are."

Paulette interrupts, "I guess, since you guys were together *all the time* and, well, Aimée is French, and you know how kissy, kissy French people are, someone must have gotten the wrong impression."

"I'm sure that's what happened," I say with a stern look on my face.

"But you must know, that if it had happened, it would be okay with us, right, Dana?" Paulette adds as Dana nods.

Me and Aimée? Well, let's just say it was more than making out. I don't tell the twins that, of course, but the thought sends shivers up my spine. They finally get their textbooks and we start on problem four. I attempt to focus on the math and even pound some numbers into my calculator, but my mind is elsewhere. My mind is on Aimée, oh beautiful Aimée. How I miss her.

Aimée is the kind of girl that you cannot help liking. She is pretty. She is sweet. She is fun. I still remember the day she introduced herself in my English class, "*Aló*, evreybudy. *Je m'apelle*, my name is Aimée. I am Aimée, I am from Calais."

My classmates all looked at each other, confusion on their faces until I said, "Calais, France, right?" Aimée smiled at me and added, "Oui, three *heures* from Paris." Her accent, her face. She was not the first girl I had felt attracted to. No, it was better than that; she was the first girl who was *actually* attracted to me.

Aimée was seated right next to me. Why? Because I was the "best English student and I would be a great help to her." Our teacher's words. Aimée and I hit it off right away and were together all the time.

Aimée was the only person I wanted near me when Glo died. Aimée and Glo never met. When Aimée arrived at Immaculate, my sister was already living at the hospital, and my parents pretty much were too. So I was on my own most of the time. Having Aimée by my side was comforting.

Aimée would come over and we would do homework together. She would make *crêpes* or strawberry *savarins* to distract me. It was precisely after tasting one of her Nutella *crêpes* that *it* happened. I remember tasting it and saying, "Oh my God, Aimée, this is so delicious, Glo is going to love it." I realized what I had said and burst into tears. Aimée pulled me close to her. I tried to stop crying; I tried to calm myself, but Aimée kept saying, "Cry, Marí, cry, please."

Marí, that's how she pronounced my name. Aimée held me close, stroked my back, and caressed my hair. I could hear her crying too.

"*Je ne c'est pas.* I don't know, I probably don't know what you feel, Marí, but if *ma soeur*, my sister, if something happened to Adelaide, I don't know what I would do." There we were. Both crying. Crying for my sister and crying for her sister who was so, so far away.

I don't know how it happened exactly. I don't know which of us started it, but a minute later we were kissing each other on the cheeks and forehead, and suddenly on the lips. I wanted to stop but, at the same time, I didn't. Aimée's lips were so sweet and soft and comforting. We never really did it,

Aimée and me, but I can say we did many things together and to each other.

* * *

"Where are you, Herrera? Is your mind taking a shower before Sister Theresa finds you?"

"Shut up!" I squeal. I grab Dana's calculator and throw it at her. The surprise attack knocks her off the bed and we break into hysterical laughter.

Part of me believes that if I told them about Aimée and me, they would understand, or at least they would try to. But I can't. I don't have the balls. Maybe Dana and Paulette have been thinking for a while that I fooled around with Aimée. Maybe that's why they were telling me they had pretty cousins for me to meet at their Sweet Sixteen party.

We continue working on the math for a while, until Dana and I take a break to tell Paulette about what happened in class the other day. We give her the play-by-play of Sister Helen's "Masturbation equals sin" lesson. We laugh and gossip for a bit before I decide it is time for me to leave. I text Dad and ask him to pick me up.

I say good-bye to Dana and Paulette. Today was a great day after all. I haven't laughed so hard in a long, long time. Not since my life began disintegrating into a shitty, hot mess.

* * *

To: aimeedelphy98@gmail.com
From: mari_herr@gmail.com
Subject: Miss ya!

Dear Aimée,

It's late. I just came back from the twins' house. You remember them, right? What am I saying, who can forget those two?

We were doing homework, it was kinda fun. They made me laugh. But they also made me realize how much I miss you.

I miss you, I miss you. You leaving is like losing Glo all over again. I mean, it is obviously not the same, because you still exist, you are somewhere in the world, but that somewhere in the world is way too far from me. I know we still have this, e-mailing each other, sharing pictures and stuff, but it's not the same.

Hey, have you given some thought to Facebook? I know you hate it and all, but if you open your account we would be able to stay in touch all the time.

Please, please, please, think about it.

xoxo

CHAPTER TWO
new old barrio

I'S GOOD FRIDAY AND WE'RE DRIVING TO LA WITH Dad. He goes almost every other weekend, but he usually goes without us. He thought it would be a good idea for all of us to go and check out the barrio and our new *old* home. We haven't been there all together for years.

Dad bought the house where grandma lived a long time ago. It's actually the place where I was born and where my parents raised me and Glo before we all moved to Santa Barbara. It's huge. "Too big for me," Grandma Sarita says all the time. My parents tried to convince her to move with us to Santa Barbara many times, but she always refused.

"This is my home, *de aquí me sacan hasta que me muera*," which means, "You will get me out of here only when I die."

Super, super dramatic, I know, right? I guess it's because of all those telenovelas Grandma watches every day. Any time she gets a cold and she is, "Dying, *mijo*. I feel like I am dying, like Jesus Christ on the cross." If any of us loses a bit of weight we are, "as skinny as a branch from a lemon tree." When the weather gets a little bit warmer she is, "like a chicken in a frying pan."

Grandma Sarita came to live in the States when she was thirteen. Her father had been working in the grape fields of California for over five years before he was able to bring his family over. She says everyone was excited to come except for her. "I was afraid, *mija*," she would tell me. "I didn't speak English, and I had never left our land, back in Sinaloa." Grandma Sarita lived with her parents and her brothers near where her father worked. When her parents split up, her mother took her to live in East LA. It was here that they both started working for a *maquiladora*, making fancy dresses. She was only seventeen when she got pregnant by a boyfriend who simply disappeared.

I like Grandma Sarita. I like her way more than my mom's parents, which is not that hard at all because my mom's parents are complete assholes. As I already explained, Grandpa is a macho man and my grandma is pretty much his slave. They disapprove of every decision my parents make. Mom can never forgive them for not coming to Glo's funeral. And why didn't they come? That's simple. They believed that my sister's death was a punishment from God because of our loose lives, whatever that means. Mom was so upset. The day we buried Glo, Mom buried her parents. Grandma Sarita stayed by my mom's side, "*Mija*, you got *me* and I love you very much. We are in this together."

Grandma Sarita is without a doubt an important figure in the barrio. She is probably the best seamstress in all of East LA. She learned from her own mother and perfected her craft through years of working at the *maquiladora*. She started sewing dresses for her friends and neighbors in her home for fun. Little by little she became known. When Dad was in middle school, she opened a little shop. That shop paid Dad's way through college. Years later, when Dad started making money, he bought her the house where she's living now.

Grandma Sarita is really amazing. You show her a dress in a magazine and after just one look, she can draw the pattern and create the same exact dress for you. She has made all the dresses for the most important events in our family. She made my mother's wedding dress and the Baptism and First Communion dresses that both Glo and I wore. She made my Flower Girl dress and Glo's Señorita dress for the annual Fiesta of Santa Barbara. She also did Glo's Sweet Sixteen dress. It was the last thing she made for her. She didn't even get to wear it. There was no big party for her, she was too sick.

It's like Mom and I are telepathic, thinking

the same thing when she tells me, "I was thinking Mari . . . Mari? Take off your headphones." Mom touches my leg to get my attention.

"What is it?"

"I was thinking, you should ask your grandma to make you a dress for the twins' Sweet Sixteen."

"How do you . . . ?"

"I saw the invitation in the mail. You're going, aren't you?"

"I don't know, I thought you wouldn't want me to because you don't like them, and you don't want me going to parties and stuff." After Glo died, she got really protective of me and wouldn't let me go out much with the girls from school.

"Nonsense," Dad says. "You've been a hermit the last couple of months, you should go."

My mom adds with a smile, "Yes, besides, I am sure you want to hang out with your friends before we move."

Now I understand why they both want me to

go. They feel guilty, guilty for forcing me to leave my life in Santa Barbara to live in a stupid barrio.

"Well, I wasn't planning on going. We'll see." I put my headphones on again and turn up the volume of the iPod. I'm in a Belle and Sebastian mood. They were Glo's favorite band.

We used to come to LA more often when Glo and I were in elementary school. We would leave early in the morning, have breakfast at this old Belgian waffle place right off the highway and spend the day at Grandma's. We would walk around the barrio, and go to the *mercadito* or to buy bread at the *panadería*. But as we started growing up, both Glo and I stopped wanting to go as often. We preferred to stay home, watch TV, and play video games while Yolanda, our maid, watched over us.

I wish things would get better for us soon because I don't want to move. I don't want to leave my life in Santa Barbara; Santa Barbara is all I know. Santa Barbara is the place where Glo and I grew up. The whole city reminds me of her. The beach reminds me of her. The mountains remind me of her. The streets. The trees. The sky. Glo is everywhere.

Thinking of Glo makes my eyes tear up. I close them and lie down on the backseat and listen to Belle and Sebastian sing.

"Mari, we're almost there. Mari, wake up," Mom says as she shakes my arms. I sit up and look through the window. I hear Elvis Presley's "Burning Love" playing on Dad's favorite radio station and see the sad gray sky of LA welcoming me. I stretch my arms and legs and notice a newspaper on my mother's lap. She has circled lots of ads in the classified section. I remember her telling me about an interview.

"What's this? You still looking for a job? I thought you had gotten that one?"

"Which one, sweetie?"

"The one in that health services company. The one here in LA."

"No, not yet. I have an interview. It's in two weeks. It seems they are in no hurry."

"Are we in a hurry?

"What do you mean?"

"It's just that you've been pretty intense with this job search."

"Well, no, but it will be best for me to find something soon."

"Didn't you say we are fine, that we have savings?"

Dad turns off Elvis from the radio and says, "Mari, we do have savings, and we will be selling the house, so even without jobs we would be fine for quite some time . . . "

"Then why do we have to freaking move to the freaking barrio?" I yell.

Mom turns around to look at me, "Because we have to, Mari. Because sometimes you have to press the restart button of your life in order to keep going."

Is that what we are doing, then? I guess we are restarting our lives after everything that has happened. "*Un mal tras otro,*" Grandma Sarita would say, "One problem after another."

We have arrived. Grandma is at the door before Dad puts the car in park. It's like she's been standing and waiting this whole time, looking out the peephole, anxiously waiting for us to get there. "*Bienvenidos.* Welcome, welcome."

I haven't seen her since my sister's funeral. I've been very selfish, but I had a good reason. When Aimée and I got closer and we started making out, all I wanted was to be with her. I knew she had to leave at the end of the semester so I had to make the most of the time we had together.

"*Mira nada más, qué grande está la Mari.* She is so tall now, not a little girl anymore."

"Grandma, since when have I been a little girl?" I ask her. See, I have always been very tall, taller than everyone else in my class. I am actually almost as tall as my dad.

"Come, give me a hug." She reaches for me with her cane in one hand.

Grandma Sarita gives me a strong hug and kisses my forehead. "*Preciosa,* how I've missed you!" *Preciosa* is what Grandma calls me. Glo was *Hermosa.* Both nicknames are different ways of calling someone beautiful. "Ready to see your new room? *Pásale,*" Grandma asks me but before we get inside, Dad says, "Mama I think we need to repaint the whole house."

"Yes, Sarita, especially now that the roof is finished. It looks great, doesn't it?" Mom says.

Grandma Sarita ignores them and walks me in. She whispers to me, "Ay, your parents—*muy* broke, *muy* broke, but they keep investing in the house. The house is fine as it is, don't you think?"

"Well, I heard it was raining inside."

"Nonsense. That is just your Aunt Angela exaggerating again."

Grandma Sarita walks me inside her house. We go to the room that used to be her mother's. It's empty now.

"Angela and I took everything out. Some things

were sent to the storage; some others I gave away. What you think? You like it, *mija*?"

"Of course, Grandma." I say, "It's perfect. I will be able to bring *most* of my furniture."

"Most?" she exaggerates her surprise, "You don't think everything will fit here? Your dresser and your bed and . . . "

"Yeah, yeah, I'm sure, but I also have my desk and my bookcases and my reading chair . . . "

"*Ay, la* bookworm. I forget that you are our family's philosopher," she pokes fun at me. "*Ay*, I have an idea! Why don't you use the shop, make it your own studio room."

The shop is a little apartment next to Grandma's house. That's where she used to work and meet her clients. There's no way my parents would let me take it.

"Your shop?" I ask her, "But that's *your* place of work."

"*Ay, mija*, I barely use it anymore. The shop is closed. I can move my stuff to this room. We will talk all about this later—now come, come, I have made *enfrijoladas*. Your favorite."

I don't say anything, but I know Grandma Sarita has confused me for Glo again. The *enfrijoladas* were Glo's favorite, not mine. I'm an enchiladas girl.

Mom and Dad join us in the kitchen. Grandma has a big table in the dining room, but just like at our house, it's only used on special occasions. Grandma cooks to order. She fries all the tortillas, shreds the chicken, the brisket, and the cheese, then makes the sauce, but it isn't until after we are all sitting at the table that she starts putting together each plate, one after the other.

She serves me first. She says, *"Enfrijoladas para la Hermosa."* *Hermosa*, that is Glo, not me. My parents look at each other and then at me, like expecting me to say something. "Smells delicious," is all I say.

I'm not lying. I can't wait to dig into the big dish with three rolled tortillas filled with shredded chicken and smothered with a thick sauce of black bean, fresh cheese and sour cream on top. *Enfrijoladas* may not be my favorite, but I do like them.

Grandma Sarita had a stroke soon after Glo died and she hasn't been the same since. She forgets dates, names, everything. That's why Dad hired a live-in nurse, Vicky. According to Dad, Vicky has become more than Grandma's nurse. They go grocery shopping, take walks around the barrio, and go to the movies. Grandma and Vicky have even started sewing together while watching telenovelas. "Vicky sounds like Grandma's girlfriend," I said once, but my joke went ignored.

Vicky has the weekends off so is not here today. Something that my dad does not like. He believes Grandma should not be left alone. Ever.

"Well, why haven't you started eating?" Grandma asks when she comes to the table with Mom's enfrijoladas plate.

"I was waiting for everyone to . . . "

"*Nada, nada, nada,*" Grandma says. "*A comer*

que se enfría." She urges me to eat before my plate gets cold.

"So, Sarita," Mom starts, "are you sewing much these days?" We can all see Grandma Sarita putting together the last plate of *enfrijoladas,* which is for my dad. Oh, I haven't mentioned that Grandma doesn't eat with us. She either eats before everyone else or after everybody is done. It has always been an issue in the family. Dad is used to it. He grew up under the care of these two very traditional women, his mother and his grandmother. But Mom, she hates it. She hates to be eating while Grandma is going here and there, bringing the salt, the cheese, pouring *agua fresca* into our glasses.

"Not really. Only for special clients and special occasions," Grandma answers once she has given Dad his plate.

"Oh," Mom says.

"Why, what do you need?" Grandma asks.

Before Mom says anything I go, "My friends,

Dana and Paulette, are having their Sweet Sixteen party soon."

"They are both celebrating it on the same day?" Grandma asks.

"They're twins."

Grandma nods, and then looks at me. "Why don't you look excited, then?" Grandma asks me and she suddenly realizes that I am not Glo, but Mari. Grandma looks at my plate and sees that it's me eating the food she made for Glo. But she says nothing.

"I don't even know if I'm going."

"Of course you're going," Mom says. "You said they're your best friends since Aimée left." It seems she forgot that she doesn't like them.

"Aimée," Grandma asks. "Who's Aimée?"

"You met her," I explain. "That French girl who was my friend, the one who came as an exchange student. She left in December. She went back to France." I see the blank look on Grandma's face and I am sure she has no clue who am I talking about.

"The one who made all those *crêpes* for us last winter," Mom adds. "Blonde girl with super curly hair."

Grandma pretends she knows who we're talking about, but I can see in her face that she is still lost.

"Oh, yes, of course. What did you say happened to her?"

"She went back home to France," I repeat.

"Oh, good for her," Grandma says. "But what does Aimée have to do with everything?" Grandma's face looks confused. "What were we talking about?"

"We were talking about your granddaughter's friends, who have invited her to their Sweet Sixteen party." Dad explains.

"Which granddaughter?" Grandma asks, perplexed by the thought that she should know and frustrated that she cannot remember. I don't want her to feel bad, so without knowing exactly what to say I try to create an alternate truth, "Well me, your favorite, of course. What do you think we should make for such special occasion, Grandma?" I may have made things even weirder. Her favorite grand-daughter, yeah right.

We all know that Glo was her very favorite. Not that she showed a different kind of love for me and Glo. It's just that everybody in the family will agree that Gloria was just better than me in so many ways. She was smarter and prettier. Glo would sit quietly at Grandma's table for hours, doing her nails, reading a book, or something girly-ish. Me? I would be running all over the house, climbing trees, or watching TV with the volume really loud.

"Well, when you're done eating, we can check some magazines. Maybe we can even go get some fabric later today," Grandma says.

"Sounds like a plan. Maybe we can even go and buy some *pan dulce* too." I love Mexican pan dulce from the kickass bakery around the corner.

"Excellent." Grandma says, "Oh, by the way, I was thinking . . . my old shop could be a perfect room for Maria here."

I hate to be called Maria. I hate Maria. It's such

a common name. It's so *Look at me and appreciate the Hispanic heritage in me.* I go by Mari. It's short and easy. It's more me.

"What?" Mom and Dad ask at the same time.

"Nothing, nothing, we will all talk about it later, now, dig in," Grandma says as she finally sits down with us. She smiles at all of us, and then stares at the empty chair by my side. Glo is here even when she is not here.

Mom and Dad, measuring tape in hand, size up the empty rooms in Grandma's house. They're trying to figure out what they will be able to bring from our place in Santa Barbara. Mom says that anything we can't bring, we can either sell or put in storage.

Grandma and I check out some dresses in one of the pattern magazines she gets in the mail every month. I tell her the party's theme is the fifties. She smiled and says, "Oh, I know what we can do then." She takes one of the magazines and flips quickly through the pages. She finds the perfect dress on the perfect model. I'm not all that femme, but that dress makes me want to be a girl in a fairytale. Grandma knows her business.

"This dress, with a crazy-looking fabric, would be *tremendo* for you," Grandma offers. *Tremendo*, I like the word. *Tremendous*. Like a bomb exploding with awesomeness.

"*Tremendo*, yes Grandma. But what do you mean by crazy-looking fabric?" I ask.

"You know, colorful flowers or a geometric pattern. *¿Me entiendes?*"

Yeah, I get it. It's a great plan.

"The store won't close till five p.m. Let's go now so we can have enough time to look around."

"We're going to the bakery, too, right?"

"*Claro.*"

After Grandma and I buy a wonderful fabric in a fun, lemon-yellow color for my dress, we walk around. She tries to show me around the barrio. She confuses places, points here and there. "*Ay, me movieron todo*," she says because the fruit store is now a taco place, and the old taco place is now a tamale store. "Well, you get the idea," she adds.

"Don't worry, Grandma, I remember some of it."

"All of this seems new to you, *nuevito*, I am sure," she says. "I will teach you your way around here because this is your new old barrio now."

This new old barrio is certainly not the place where I want to be.

"There's the bakery. You do remember it, right, *Preciosa*?"

"You bet I do."

This bakery has always been my personal favorite. I could get here even with my eyes closed, the sweet smell of sugar guiding my way. This was the only place we were allowed to come on our own, back when we were kids and came to visit Grandma

Sarita. Dad or Grandma would give us a five dollar bill to get anything we wanted. Glo and I would buy *conchitas*, donuts—tons of donuts, croissants—only here they are called *cuernitos*—empanadas, turnovers, *polvorones*—which are like a sugar shortbread—*tres leches* cake, and my all time favorites, *marranitos*— delicious gingerbread in the shape of a pig.

The place looks a bit different than I remember. The cupboards are also new and fancy. They still have that old cash register but next to it you can see an iPad and a Square system, too, for people who pay with a card.

My Grandma grabs a tray and tongs. I stand in the middle of the store, close my eyes, and take a deep breath. Childhood memories come flooding back while the sugary smell invades my senses. My mouth is watering; I can almost taste . . .

"Hey, *muévete chica,*" a strong deep voice calls from behind.

"What?" I open my eyes and notice a girl, about

my age, but shorter than me, holding a loaded tray of conchitas.

"*¿Me deja pasar la dama?*" Which is an odd question, especially for someone of my own age. She was asking to get by, but in a very formal Spanish not commonly used.

"*Sí, sí. Lo siento,*" I apologize. My Spanish sounds horrible; I haven't practiced it in years. Anyone could tell. This girl notices my accent and makes fun of me.

"*Lou sientou,*" she mocks, adding an extra *u* sound at the end of my vowels. "So, you moving or not?" she adds when I don't let her pass. She's smaller than me, but has much more attitude. Her flour-covered apron doesn't hide her mannish clothes. She's wearing khaki Dickies and a long-sleeved shirt all buttoned up. I step aside, and as she walks by me, I notice her pair of white Jordans.

Jordans—how much I begged my mom to buy me a pair not so long ago. "No way," she said.

"Those are men's tennis shoes." I wanted them so bad.

"Doña Sarita, long time no see," I hear someone greeting my grandma.

"Don Felipe, *¿qué tal?* Look, this is my grand-daughter, *mi nieta*—do you remember Maria?" Grandma beckons to me. I walk to her, hating every letter of my name.

"Of course. How are you, *chiquita?*"

"Not *Chiquita* anymore. I've grown up."

Don Felipe and Grandma Sarita laugh. Then he yells to the woman at the cash register, "*Margarita, a Doña Sarita aquí y a su nieta no les cobres.*" He tells her not to charge us.

The girl who was carrying the tray is now at the cupboard. I can see her face and hear her whisper, "Goodwill much?"

"So you visiting your grandma?" Don Felipe asks me. Grandma answers for me, "No, she and her parents will be moving back to LA."

"And you are in, what, high school?" Don Felipe asks me

"Yes, I'll be a junior this fall," I respond, but I don't even look at him. I can't stop staring at the girl working with the tray of conchitas.

"She'll be going to Garfield, I think."

Don Felipe says, "Oh, no Doña Sarita, you have to send her to César Chávez. It's closer and better than Garfield." He then points at the girl with the conchitas and says, "My Natalia goes to César Chávez, she can tell you all you need to know. Natalia, get over here."

Natalia pretends not to hear her father; she continues putting away the trays with conchitas.

"Natalia? Natalia come here."

"*What?* I am busy. You told me I have to be one hundred percent focused, remember?" Natalia has a strong deep voice. She's not exactly pretty, but there's something about her—something attractive. She has two piercings on her dimples. I wonder if they hurt when she smiles. Her big brown eyes are highlighted by thick black eyeliner. Oh, and she has the thinnest eyebrows I've ever seen. I wonder if she is goth or something?

"Come here, Natalia," says Don Felipe. "Tell these ladies about your school." Natalia pushes away the pastry tray and walks towards us.

"What do you want me to say, *Pá*?"

"Look, this is . . . I'm sorry, I forgot your name," Don Felipe tells me.

"Mari, my name is Mari." Her eyes look me over head to toe before saying, "Mari or Maria? Your Grandma here just called you Maria, I heard her."

"I prefer Mari."

"Maria it is then," Natalia says.

Don Felipe continues, "Mari will be moving here, Natalia. Tell her about your school."

"Well," she starts, "classes suck, but most of the teachers are okay. The school is kinda new so it doesn't smell like piss. Oh, and we don't like *blancas* like you."

"Natalia!" Don Felipe gives her an elbow to the side.

"Well, it's true."

I ignore her comment and pull her aside. I ask her, "That school, does it really smell like piss? Mine smells like incense and candles mixed in with a little bit of old lady, because of the nuns."

"Nuns?" Natalia uncrosses her arms and goes, "Are you in a Catholic school or something?"

"Yeah."

"That sucks."

"Big time," I say. Natalia and I exchange smiles. Maybe she doesn't dislike me?

"I would die in that *clecha*. I would die . . . or I would kill a nun, I swear."

"*Clecha?* What's that?" I ask.

"School."

"Oh, is that Spanish?"

"Sorta."

"How 'bout *colegio* then?"

"*Colegio*, yes, but that's for snobs."

"Oh, my *colegio* is full of those. Believe me," I say.

"Aren't you one too?"

"Not at all."

"But you prefer to be called Mari rather than Maria. Doesn't that make you a bit of a snob?"

"No."

"Mmmh. Anyway, how do you survive the *monjitas*?"

Monjitas. I had never heard this word before. Let's see, I know *monjas* mean nuns. I know *-ita* is a diminutive. So literally *monjitas* would mean little nuns. But the thing with Spanish is that if you add a diminutive like *-ita* or *-ito* to a noun, it doesn't necessarily mean small or little, it's more of a derogatory thing.

"It's not that bad. You get used to them. You have to pray in the first class of the day and attend Mass once a week. Believe me, that is the one thing I will not miss when we move here."

"How 'bout your *clica*?"

"My what?"

"Your friends, will you miss your friends?"

"Yeah, I guess."

"Mari, we should get going," Grandma calls, cutting into our conversation.

I don't want to leave; I want to keep talking to Natalia.

"Take some *cochitos*, they just came out of the oven," Natalia says as she goes back to work on her trays. It's my turn to look her over. I take a glance at her tennis shoes one more time and can't help saying, "I love your Jordans."

Natalia turns back to me, she takes a look at her own shoes and says, *"Rifan, ¿verdad?"*

"Rifan? What does that mean?" I ask Natalia.

"They're badass, *rifan.*"

Grandma and I buy the bread and some milk. We say *"Adiós"* to Don Felipe. Natalia looks at me and says, "Welcome to your new barrio."

I ask Grandma more about Don Felipe and his daughter, "It seems you and he are good friends, right?"

"*Pues te diré*, not really. He's always very polite with me so I am as polite as he is, but I don't like him all that much—*es un viejo cabrón*. But one thing I will give you, he makes the best bread in the barrio."

"He does." I say as I take a bite of my *cochito*. "What does *viejo cabrón* mean?"

Grandma looks at me and after thinking for a few minutes says, "An asshole, *pues*."

* * *

To: aimeedelphy98@gmail.com
From: mari_herr@gmail.com
Subject: How I Survived a Double Sweet Sixteen

Dear Aimée,

So last weekend it was the twins' birthday. They turned sixteen, and as you know, turning sixteen here is a big deal. You have to have a big party, you get to wear a nice elegant dress and just show off. For guys, it's just another birthday, so they couldn't give a shit about it, of course.

The twins' mother took it seriously. She organized a kickass party. I wasn't sure my parents would let me go, but they did, and although you know I am more of a hermit, I went and I had so much fun. Let me give you the highlights of the event:

1) The decorations, everyone's clothes, and the music was all 60s-themed. It was incredible, it was like all out of an Audrey Hepburn movie.

2) Dana and Paulette looked like rockabilly girls with their polka-dot dresses and hairdos. Paulette's dress was black and white and Dana's was red and white.

3) We all had one, ONE, mimosa for the twins' toast.

4) The guys in the band were all dressed like James Dean (and if you don't know who James Dean is, go and Google his name).

5) Lots of guys and girls started out on the dance floor, but by the end it was only the girls dancing without shoes.

6) The party ended at 2 a.m. Everybody left but me and a few other girls. The twins' mom had invited us to stay for an after-party, and she had enough food to feed an army. We played some music 'til 5 or 6 in the morning.

I wish you had been there, Aimée.

Since you left, and since I quit the soccer team, I've been hanging out with the twins. I can't say we are BFFs, but we've become close friends. Can you believe they asked about you and me?! I didn't tell them anything, of course. I wonder if anyone else at school thinks you and me, well, that we were more than friends.

Well, gotta go now. Write me soon.

xoxo, Mari.

CHAPTER THREE
smells like sugar spirit

I SPENT MOST OF OUR LAST FEW WEEKS IN SANTA Barbara at the beach sunbathing like a lizard. When I wasn't at the beach, Mom made me work my ass off downsizing everything in our closets, kitchen, etc.

We moved in with Grandma last week. Uncle Robert lent us a truck and had some of the employees from his furniture store help us out. Some of our stuff went to storage, but the rest we have to find room for at Grandma's house. Mom wants Grandma to sell or give away the things in her living room and dining room so we can put our Santa Barbara stuff in there. Dad doesn't think Mom should ask her to do that. He says it would offend Grandma. I agree.

It's not clear to me if we're going to be living with her for a while, until our house in Santa Barbara is sold and we can buy something else, or if we are staying here for good. I don't want to ask because right now I cannot say a thing to Mom. She's in a bad mood.

Mom isn't happy at all that the shop will be my room. She says it's completely inappropriate for a girl to live away from home before she is old enough. Come on! She wants to open a wall so she can come into my room from hers. "*Nada de eso,*" Grandma said, "Mari will be just fine."

I admire Grandma for standing up to Mom—it takes guts. I love my new room. I had no idea I would like it this much. And well, my room in our old home kicked ass with those big windows and the bathroom, but this one, I don't know, it has some coziness. Vicky, Grandma's caregiver, helped me clean and paint it. I like Vicky. She's this big strong woman with the softest voice on earth. She comes three days a week. She's all butchy and I wonder if she is gay. I don't dare ask. If Paulette were here she would have asked already.

We text every day, me and the twins. I don't get to miss them, texting with them all day long is like being around them.

What else is new? Uncle Robert convinced Dad to accept the job; he hates it, of course. Mom, on the other hand, got that health services job she was aiming for. She says it's the first time she feels that she is actually doing something to help the community. And this definitely has taken away some of the stress in our family. Translation: if Mom is stressed we all end up stressed, if Mom is happy we all feel happy.

Anyway, it's a time of new beginnings. My parents have new jobs, and me, well, I am officially a César Chávez High School student. I registered last Friday. The school is not so bad. As soon as we came in I noticed something, something strange.

It took me a few minutes to realize what it was. Noisy, that's what César Chávez was, noisy. Silence reigns at Immaculate, which can be hard to believe considering it's an all-girls school. Looking back, it felt more like a convent.

At César Chávez, Mom and I heard conversations, laughter, and gossip, in both English and Spanish. And everyone is *so* friendly. Everyone was willing to help us out and show us around the school.

I was hoping to see that girl again, the one from the bakery, Natalia. But she was nowhere to be found. I did meet a girl who will be in some of my classes, Rita. She told me all about the school, the people, the sports and clubs. "I was in soccer the first year, but then I found my one *pasión*." Rita joined the orchestra, she plays the violin. "My Papa doesn't say anything, but I think he liked it better when I was in soccer." Rita is from El Salvador. She was brought to the US when she was five years old.

As we were leaving, Mom told me, "I see you found yourself a new friend."

"Who, her? She's okay. She used to be on the soccer team."

"Is that right?"

"Yeah. I miss soccer."

Mom stopped walking, stood in front of me and said, "Well, why don't you give it a try, Mari? Maybe it's time."

"Yeah, maybe."

"We would be very happy to see you back on the field, you know? Your Dad and me."

* * *

To use Rita's words, soccer is my one pasión. I started practicing when I was nine years old. But I started learning all about it when I was six or seven, thanks to my dad, who is the greatest fan ever. I play defense, just like he did when he was in high school.

Glo didn't understand soccer all that much. She found it funny that I was a defender. "It sounds like you are a superhero."

"I am. I get to protect the ball," I would tell her.

"So you are like a seeker?"

"A seeker? Oh my god, Gloria. Quidditch doesn't actually exist!"

"It doesn't?" she would say, faking surprise. "Well, tell me again what a defender does besides protect the ball from the enemy."

"It's pretty simple, but you wouldn't understand," I would say in my teaching-a-seminar voice

Glo wasn't into sports whatsoever. She was all about the arts. She would dance, sing, even act. But as much as she didn't like soccer, she would always come to my games with my parents.

Vicky is helping me finish up my room today—hanging stuff on the walls, organizing books on the shelves. I hear a knock at the door.

"Ready for next week?" Grandma Sarita asks me as she walks in.

I turn to see her, and then I throw myself dramatically on the bed. "Not at *all*," I yell.

Grandma laughs and sits right next to me. "*Ni yo, mija*, we are so not ready for you to not be around all day," Grandma says, "Right, Vicky? Who are we going to gossip with after watching *The View* or our telenovela? Your Dad?"

"*No creo*, I don't think so," Vicky adds. "It seems like Don Samuel hates a good drama."

"*Ay no*, I didn't realize I'm gonna miss *Amor de Mis Amores*, Grandma. What am I going to do? It's the only telenovela I actually like."

"We will keep you posted, don't worry," says Grandma.

"Or maybe, maybe we can get that thing that records shows—what is it called?" Vicky asks me.

"There's no way my parents would get us that. It seems like their downsizing is all about taking the fun out of our lives."

"Oh, well, at least we have *donas*, which is why I

came. Do you wanna take a walk with me and then go to the bakery?"

Of course I wanted to go, not just to get out for a bit, but also for sugar, delicious empty calories, and the chance to see Natalia again.

"You guys go. I will finish here," Vicky says. "Have you taken your pills, Sarita?" Grandma makes a childish face and says no.

"Let's go get them, then," Vicky says as she walks Grandma out of my room.

"I'll put my shoes on and meet you at the gate, Grandma."

I open my closet. This should be easy. I should just reach out for whatever is down there—sandals, tennis shoes, anything—and simply put them on. Instead, I sit down and look at my shoes one by one. Which pair should I wear? Shoes can be the best and worst way to impress someone. Not that I wanna impress Natalia, I mean, who knows if she will actually be there, but . . . Ha, who am I trying to fool? I do wanna impress her. I do want her to notice me, but we are talking about a girl who has the most amazing Jordans. What do I have to wear that will impress her? Not my rich-girl Toms for sure, my purple Havaianas are also out of the question . . .

"*Lista*, sweetie? You ready?" I hear Grandma yelling.

"Just a sec," I yell back.

Fuck. What should I wear? I stand up and look at myself in the mirror to see what exactly I got going on. White cargo shorts and a pink "I ♥ CALIFORNIA" shirt. Cute. Too cute. I take the shirt off and put on a black shirt with a punked-out Emily Dickinson. Yes, perfect. I could wear my red Converse. They are old and worn and they will give me a casual badass look. I mean if the casual badass looks exists at all.

Jesus, this is stupid. What am I doing? We're not even friends.

* * *

We walk along Third Street for a while. Grandma's been telling me a story about her childhood in Sinaloa. She used to live in a small town near Mazatlán, the famous beach in the north of Mexico.

"In the summers, my brothers and I would go to Mazatlán to sell necklaces made of *conchitas*, sea shells, that my mom would make. Because it was summer, there were more *gringo* tourists, you know? We got paid in dollars."

"And then what did you do with the money?"

"Well, of course, we had to give our earnings to Mom. My dad was already here in the States, working, and he wasn't always able to send us money, so we had to provide for ourselves."

"Right."

"But Mother would give one dollar to each of us. Uff, how many candies you could buy with one dollar back then. Tons—tons of candies. *Tamarindos*, *mazapanes* . . . ufff."

My grandma turns into a little girl as she gives

me a long list of the candies she and her brother would buy with their money.

"Those were good times."

"Sounds like the way Glo and I felt when we spent our money at the bakery," I say, but she doesn't hear me. She's somewhere else. She's a kid in Mazatlán with her brothers.

We are almost two blocks from the bakery. My heart is beating fast. We hear the thump, thump of a skateboard coming behind us. It's her. It's Natalia.

She yells: "Coming through, *permiso, permiso.*"

Both my grandma and I get out of the way. She is wearing the same Dickies she was wearing the last time I saw her and a white shirt. I get a hint of sugar as she passes right next to me, but I am probably wrong.

Natalia arrives before we do, obviously. She gets off her board and her father comes out the door.

We cannot hear what he's saying, but by the looks of it, he seems to be preaching to her. Natalia doesn't seem to care. She just steps on the tail of her skateboard, which jumps and lands in her left hand. Impressive. As she gets in the store, Don Felipe sees us.

"*Doña Sarita, ¡qué gusto!* How is my favorite client? Besides beautiful, of course." He is a flirt, no doubt.

"*Bien*, Don Felipe. How are you?"

"Oh, trying to not go crazy with this one who is always late," he says as he points at Natalia inside the store. "Come on in."

Don Felipe stays outside the store. I go directly to get a tray and bread tongs.

"Get some *bolillos*," Grandma says.

"Which ones are those again?"

"The long ones, the ones you call *subs* but are nothing like subs," Grandma replies while pointing to a big basket near the employee's door.

As I find my way to the *bolillos*, I hear Natalia

cursing somewhere inside. As I take one bun after another, I can't help myself and look around to find out where she is. I fail to grab one of the bolillos, and it falls on the floor, I hesitate to get it, then I hear her say, "Hurry, five second rule." Natalia grabs it with a pair of tongs.

"The five second rule? What's that?" I ask her.

"*Chica,* you don't know? Oh my god, there's so much to teach you," she says, holding my fallen bolillo. "The five second rule. Here it goes." Natalia clears her throat and starts in a serious tone, "The Five Second Rule states that in East LA, and probably any place in the world, when food drops on the ground, it will not be contaminated, and thus, will not contaminate you, if it is picked up within five seconds of falling."

"Really, it won't? Have I been fooled all these years?" I ask. Natalia nods. Then she looks at the bolillo, blows it off a little, and throws it back into the basket where she mixes it with the rest of the bread.

"Well, in case the rule has changed, let's get you another one." She smiles as she takes another bolillo from the basket and places it on my tray. "So, what's new? You moved in yet?"

"Yes. This is my first week here," I tell her.

"Cool. Which school are you going to?" Natalia asks.

"César Chávez, like you suggested," I say smiling, but my smile fades as she says,

"Chávez? Wow. Just for the record, I didn't suggest it, my father did."

"Oh, well . . . " I don't know what to say.

"Anyway, good luck and shit. Gotta work now."

I don't want her to leave, not like that. I mean we were laughing together just a second ago.

"Hey, I like your skateboard. Do you . . . " I don't even know what to ask, "Do you ride it like everywhere?"

"I would if my *Pá* let me," Natalia says as she points at Don Felipe who is now talking to an old lady and my grandma.

"He doesn't let you?"

"Of course not. He says girls shouldn't ride skateboards because, of course, he lives in the nineteenth century."

"I don't think there were skateboards in that time," I laugh.

"Well, I know *that*, I'm not stupid, but boring, old-fashioned men come from the 1800s." I'm walking behind her as she moves around the shop. "Not that I will actually obey him, of course, he also says ladies should not have piercings, tattoos, or shave their heads. But my body, my call, right?"

"Yeah." I am all smiles.

"How 'bout your folks, are they very strict too?"

"Sometimes. Hey, so have you registered already for the fall?"

"*Mi jefe* did," Natalia says as she stops at the conchitas section and starts putting bread away.

"*Jefe*?" I ask her. "Your boss did your registration?"

"My *jefe*, my old man, my boss . . . my dad, *pues*."

"Ohhh. That's what you call him?"

"No, *tonta*, that is not what *I* call him, that's what we *all* call our dads 'round here. Jeez, so much to teach you, man." I feel so, so stupid. I don't even know what to say. Maybe Natalia feels bad about her linguistics lesson because she then tells me, "Hey, that's a cool shirt. Who's that?"

"Emily Dickinson."

"Well, I can read *that*, but who is she?"

"Oh, well, only like the best modern poet in this country."

"She *does* look modern, I give you that. Is she like, young?" I can't help laughing a bit but try to refrain from doing so. I explain to her then who Emily Dickinson was.

"What are you, like an English nerd or what?"

"Nah, I just like literature a lot."

"Well, I hate it. I suck at it, suck big time. The only poet I actually like is Kurt Cobain."

"You're kidding?"

"No, I am not."

"You do know he wasn't an actual poet, he was just a composer and singer."

"And you're the literature fan? What's a composer but a poet?" She has a point.

"I guess you're right."

"Of course I am, have you ever read the lyrics of 'Smells Like Teen Spirit'?"

"I don't think so."

"Well, you gotta. It was an anthem back in its time. The title says it all, 'Smells like Teen Spirit'."

"But that's a girl's deodorant."

"It's way more than that, man." Natalia looks straight at me and reaches for my left shoulder.

I feel nervous, and when I am nervous I do or say stupid things like, "Well, you smell like sugar."

"What?"

Oh my god, did I just say that? This is so embarrassing. "Nothing."

"What did you say?"

"Nothing, I swear." Thank God, Grandma calls me at that very minute.

"Mari, did you get the *bolillos*?"

"No, not yet," I tell Grandma.

"They're over there, Maria," Natalia says. "They're probably still warm."

I wanna tell her not to call me Maria, but what's the point? I grab some sweet bread and take the tray to the cash register where Grandma pays.

I try to say bye to Natalia as we leave the store, but her back is to us and I can see she has her headphones on. I don't know what is it about her. I just can't stop looking at her hair, her ass, her Jordans. I like her. I do.

✳ ✳ ✳

To: mari_herr@gmail.com

From: aimeedelphy98@gmail.com

Subject: RE: How I Survived a Double Sweet Sixteen

Dear Mari,

You made me laugh so much with your email

about that crazy sweet sixteen party. I wish I had been there. I can't imagine how the twins will be when they get to college. Please send me pictures of the party. I wanna see the twins' dresses, but especially yours.

Aaaaand, I did open a Facebook account, but that thing is not for me. I closed it three hours later. It's overwhelming, I don't know how people do it. I think I will stick to my email account. I am such a lame romantic. Really, I wish we could go back to the time people wrote actual letters to each other, you know, hand-written letters.

Tell me more about your barrio. It sounds like an exotic place.

JTK

A.

CHAPTER FOUR
¿ habla español?

THIS IS MY SECOND WEEK AT CÉSAR CHÁVEZ. I THOUGHT that I was going to be able to understand Spanish much more by now, but I feel like a fucking idiot. Yes, *fucking*. That's the one good thing about not going to Immaculate. I can curse all the fucking time without being reported.

Anyway, in the classroom all we use is English, yes, but the fun, the jokes, *all* the jokes, that my classmates say while the teachers are distracted, well, all of those are in Spanish. And I miss it all because *No hablo español.*

Spanish is the official language at school if you're going to: 1) fight, 2) insult, 3) joke, 4) practice sports, and 5) flirt. Not that anyone is flirting with me, but I can tell when it's happening because I hear guys fooling around with girls by saying, "*Hola, chula,*" or "*¿A dónde tan solita?*" which means, "Where are you going so alone?"

Soccer practice is the most difficult. It just started last Monday and even though our coach speaks English, she uses some specific words in Spanish to lead us. Today, for example, I missed a couple of shots. She yelled, "*Ponte lista,* Herrera." Which to me means something like, "Be ready." So I told her, "Yes, I am ready." She said, "No, no, no, not be ready. *PONTE LISTA*, when the ball comes." I nodded and said, "okay," but I did not actually understand what she meant. I still don't.

Later, as I was walking off the field to get water I heard, "*Aguas,* Maria, *aguas.*" I turned around and *pum*, a ball hit my face. Natalia had kicked it. Yes, Natalia is on the team, too, which makes me a bit nervous. I could tell it was an accident, but instead of apologizing, she got all mad and said, "I did tell you to be careful, Maria. I yelled *Aguas* . . . not my problem that you don't *habla espanniool*." And that's how I know that yelling "aguas" means "watch out."

I told her, "My name is not Maria!"

"It isn't?" She pretended to be confused. "I can swear I heard you saying your name was Maria."

"It is, but I don't like it, so cut it out," I told her with a tone and an attitude I didn't know I had.

"Maria, Maria, Maria, Maria. I can't cut it out. Your name has possessed me," she said. She walked away, not without first giving me the finger, and repeating my name, "Maria, Maria, Maria."

I don't understand Natalia. Just the day before yesterday I bumped into her near the bakery. She said hi, and even chatted with me for a bit. But at school she mostly ignores me.

It's because of her friends, two girls who are grumpy and scary like bulldogs. They bark at everyone and call me names and push me around. One is tall and skinny, the other one is short and a bit chubby. They both remind me of Cinderella's sisters, Drizella and Anastasia.

Natalia is far from being a sweet Cinderella, though. She becomes a bulldog too. Well, no, more like a mean Chihuahua. You see her and you think, "Oh, how cute," but then when you get close she growls at you.

My head hurts. I just wanna stick my head under cold water. The coach sends us to the showers. Natalia has left the field before everyone. I wonder why. I wish I didn't care, but I do. I like her, I like her a *lot*. I know I just met her and everything, but since I did, well . . . how can I put this? Since that first day I saw her at the bakery, she's been on my mind. I picture her next to me as I masturbate. There, I said it.

I picture her with her shirt and Dickies, wearing her Jordans, holding me by my waist and kissing me. She has this bright red color on her lips. First she gives me small, soft kisses around my neck, like she is drawing a necklace on me. Then my ears, my cheeks, my nose. Then she lands on my lips. Her tongue wrestling with mine. I get wet, so wet, just thinking about it now. I imagine my face with her lipstick marks all over it.

I used to think I wasn't what I am. I used to think that I liked people for who they were, and it was just coincidence that they all happened to be women. But then Aimée happened. And Aimée made me realize that I had been crushing on girls.

I haven't talked about it with anyone except Aimée. Aimée understood it because she's a lesbian too. An experienced one. I wouldn't say Aimée and I were a couple; she made it very clear that we weren't. We were just friends, close friends, too close maybe.

"Aimée. Who the hell is Aimée?" Natalia is standing next to me in the girls showers. It seems like somehow I managed to let Aimée's name slip from my lips. Normally I would not know what to say. Instead, it seems a new Mari emerges again and replies, "Someone you don't know. Why? You jealous?" Natalia gives me a look like saying, "What the fuck?" She even blushed. She looks around, making sure no one is close by.

"Shut up, Maria," Natalia says, "You gotta be careful here." She starts walking away. She's wrapped in a towel, which allows me to see her beautiful bare shoulders.

"Hey," I call her, but she ignores me. "Natalia, I'm talking to *you*."

"What do you want?" she asks without looking at me. I follow her to the lockers where she grabs her clothes. Her hair is a wet mess.

"Can we talk?"

Natalia looks around, the rest of the girls are either coming out of the showers or finishing up dressing. No one is paying attention to us. She then goes, without looking at me, "What do you want, *Mari*?"

"Oh, now you call me Mari?"

"Isn't that what the Lady wants to be called?"

"Well, no, not like that, you're just making fun of me."

"Fine. Ma-ri. Better?" she says, faking some sorta British accent.

"You know what? Don't call me anything at all." Natalia looks at me, surprised. Without taking her eyes off me she puts on her underwear.

I pretend I'm not uncomfortable watching her do this, and continue, "Anyway, tell me why . . . why are you like this with me at school?"

"Like what?" Natalia asks while drying herself off before putting on her clothes. Dickies, undershirt, shirt, socks.

"Like you don't know me."

"Well. I don't, do I?"

"Yes, you do."

"Are you sure? You don't even remember we met when we were kids."

"What?" For a second I don't understand what she's talking about, but then it clicks. Her dad, Don Felipe, did say that Natalia and I used to play together when we were little. I ask her, "And *you* do?"

"Of course I do. You were such a *lloroncita,* a total whiner."

Lloroncita. A little whiner. *Lloroncita.* It's as if a screen has just dropped in front of me playing a movie of my sister and me with some other kids at a park near my Grandma's. We're playing tag, but I am "it" most of the time, so I get mad and start crying. They all start calling me *lloroncita.*

"Hey, you hear me? Hello?" Natalia asks. I leave behind the *lloroncita* in me and say, "And is that why you are so mean to me? Because I don't remember you? I don't understand. Just the other day you and I were talking about music, right outside your bakery," I say strongly, even though inside, my own tone surprises me.

"No, it's not that. I mean, it's nothing. You wouldn't understand. Anyway, I am talking to you, aren't I?" She sounds nervous for the first time.

"Well, yeah, but you kicked the ball at my face, remember?"

"Ay, that was an accident, and you know it. Look I gotta run to work or *mi jefe* will . . . "

"Kick you in the face?" I say.

"*Ganas tiene*, he wishes to." Natalia is now putting her stuff away and closing her locker. She stops for a second, and looks at me.

"Listen Maria, I mean, Mari, I mean . . . "

I interrupt her and say, "Maria, *demonios, llámame* MARIA." Look at me, I'm on fire. I'm even speaking Spanish!

"Jesus, decide once and for all what you wanna be called."

Some sort of rage possesses me, the *lloroncita* is really gone when I yell and say, "Maria, call me Maria."

"Fine, Maria. Listen, Maria, I like you. I really do, Maria, but we can't. We can't be friends. Not here, Maria." She repeats my name to annoy me, but as she does I start to find it appealing.

Maria, that's who I am now. Maria. I like the sound of it now: *Maria*.

"Why? Why can't be we friends? Is it because of your goth friends?"

Natalia bursts into laughter, "They are not goths, you idiot. They're *cholas,* not that you would understand, of course. Anyway they don't like me being friends with anyone, much less a whitey like you."

"I'm not white."

"You kinda are."

"I'm not. Look at my skin. Look at my face. Look at my hair. I'm not white."

"Well, still. We can't be friends."

"Never?"

Natalia looks at me with a stern expression. "Just not here. Okay?"

"Fine." I'm about to let her go. I'm about to forget this whole thing. But I feel a new me expanding, I am Maria now and I go, "How about texting? Can we be texting friends?"

"What do you mean?"

"I thought you were smart. Come on, let's just exchange phone numbers and we can text each other whenever we want. Unless your *jefe* hasn't gotten you a phone, of course."

Natalia looks at me. She is so serious. I feel she is going to tell me to fuck off, but then she surprises me. "I do have a phone, Maria. And texting, texting is a good idea, Maria."

"Nuff with the Maria."

"*Por fin*, Maria? Just make up your mind—what should I call you, then?"

"Oh my God, never mind. You call me whatever you want."

"Lady Maria, that's what I will call you." Natalia says, smiling.

Is she flirting with me? I wonder.

I give Natalia my number. "Maria Herrera," I tell her, but instead of writing my name she types *LM*.

"What is that?" I ask her.

"Lady Maria, duh!"

"Why?"

"Because you behave like one. I am sure you use a fork and knife to eat tortillas."

We both smile. Natalia rings me back so I can save her number. As I am about to type her name, I ask, "Everybody here calls you Rat, right?"

"Yes."

"Why?"

"It's stupid. This girl I know used to call me Ratalia instead of Natalia and one thing led to another."

"That's funny," I say, and I start typing Rat on my phone, but she stops me.

"No, Natalia is fine. I like it when people actually use my name."

"Look at you," I say, "Maybe I should call you Lady Natalia." She smiles and gives me a subtle punch on my shoulder.

She's getting ready to leave. I stop her. "Hey, why did you tell me I gotta be careful here?" Natalia stares at me and stays quiet for a second or two. Girls come and go around us, but no one is paying attention. Everyone here is talking about the practice or about this Friday's party.

Natalia goes, "Not *you*-you. People like *us*. People like you and me—*we* gotta be careful."

"Because we are Hispanic?"

"Ha, ha. No, of course not—everyone here is Hispanic. People like *us, jotas pues.*"

"*Jotas?* What's that?"

"*Lenchas. Machorras. Jotas,* you know?" she is speaking very softly.

"No, I don't."

"Ay, forgot it. *No hablo español,*" Natalia says, imitating my voice. "I will explain it to you some other day." And before leaving she says, "You're a *jota,* maybe you don't know it yet, but you are. Just like me."

* * *

Grandma fell asleep watching one of her telenovelas so it's only me and Vicky in the TV room. Mom's still at work. Dad just got back from the store and went directly to bed.

This is my chance. Commercials are on, so I take a step. "Hey, Vicky. Can I ask you something?"

"What is it, Mari?" She says without taking her eyes off the TV.

"First, promise me that you will answer me no matter what." I see that I have Vicky's attention now.

"Yes, promise, promise. What is it?"

I don't know how to start. Should I just go and say the word or should I explain the whole thing? I decide to just say it.

"What does *jota* mean?"

Vicky's face relaxes as she says, "That's how we say the letter *j* in Spanish—*jota*." Her attention returns to the TV.

"Really? Only that?"

"Yes."

That can't be it, it doesn't make sense. I decide to try again, "But what if, what if . . . I mean, imagine this context. Imagine a person who says, *people like us, jotas.* What does that mean? It can't be just the letter *j*, can it?"

Vicky turns to make sure my grandma is sleeping. She looks around, changes her position, and faces me on the sofa. "Who told you this?"

"Just someone from school."

"Why?"

"I dunno. Why Vicky? What does it mean?" Vicky wipes her lips with the palm of her hand, before saying,

"*Joto* means gay. *Él es joto*, means he is gay."

"Oh."

"Wait no, it's not the same. It is used more like an insult, like saying faggot. But if the person who says it is actually gay, well, then it is not an insult. It's just like owning it."

"Ooohh. Wait, so *joto* is for men. What about *jota*?"

"Well, that's like saying lesbian, but just the same. It can be an insult if you use it on somebody else," Vicky explains. "Now, tell me, why are you asking me this?"

"No reason."

"Come on, Mari. Why do you ask?"

"Just because," I say. The telenovela is on again. I point it out to Vicky, but she ignores me.

"Mari, tell me the truth. Did this *someone* tell you *I* was a *jota*?" Vicky's words take me by surprise.

"What? No, Vicky, not at all."

"Tell me what this person told you about me. I won't get mad."

"Vicky, I promise—no one told me anything about you. Really, this has nothing to do with you." I can see she's not satisfied with my words. She invites me to go with her to the kitchen. Once there, Vicky turns on the stove and puts the kettle on the burner. She takes out two cups and puts two spoons of instant coffee in them. She takes the milk out of the fridge and pours some in a pot before putting it on the stove. *Café con leche.*

I sit down at the table, clueless.

"Look Mari, I trust you and I'm sure you will not say anything."

"What is it, Vicky?"

"Your Grandma knows, but not your parents and, well, they're really nice but you never know."

"Vicky, I don't understand."

When we are both stirring our café con leche, she goes, "I'm a lesbian, Mari, a *jota*. But you knew this. Tell me, who told you?"

"No one, Vicky. I'm sorry. I didn't know. I don't want you to . . . "

"Fine. If you don't want to say who told you this about me, it's okay. But please don't say anything to your parents. If they have to know, I prefer it's me who tells them when the time is right."

"So Grandma knows?" I'm surprised.

"Yes, she does."

"And what did she say?"

"Well, you know her, she just said, 'As long as you take care of me and you eat my cooking, I don't care what you do or what you are, Vicky.'"

Vicky and I laugh.

"Hey, Vicky do you, you know, do you have a

101

girlfriend or something?" Vicky looks at me, her big dark eyes trying to find an answer.

"Kinda. I'm in a relationship, but because of her situation we have to keep it a secret. To everyone in her family I am just *a friend*. I'd be lucky if at some point I just get to be Tía Vicky."

I feel it's now my turn to open up with Vicky and tell her about me. I wonder where I left the set of balls I had this morning when I was with Natalia. The only thing I say is, "Vicky, thank you for confiding in me. You have nothing to worry about. I won't say a word to my parents, but they're really cool, you know? I don't think this would be a problem for them."

"You think they would still like me if I tell them I am a *jota*?"

"*¡Claro que sí!*" I say, surprised at my own Spanish.

I invite her to go back to the TV room. Grandma is awake now. She says, "Oh my god, where were you both? *Se están perdiendo todo*, you are missing the whole telenovela, you two."

Vicky and I smile and exchange looks. I know at some point I will end up doing the same, trusting my own secret with her. I will tell her, "Vicky, I am a *jota* too."

When we sit down I realize I have one more question. I wait for Grandma to doze off again, which happens in like ten seconds.

"Hey Vicky, can I ask you another question?"

"*Mija*, you can ask me anything."

"What exactly is a *chola*?" Vicky starts laughing at me, so much that Grandma wakes up for a second, looks at us and then goes back to sleep.

"Ay, Mari what's with you today? Is it Social Studies Day for you or what? A *chola*. How can I explain what a *chola* is? Let me think."

According to Wikipedia: *Cholo (Spanish pronunciation: ['tʃolo]) is an ethnic slur created by Hispanic* criollos *in the 16th century. In sociological literature, it is one of* castas, *and refers to individuals of mixed or pure Native American ancestry, or other racially mixed origin. The precise usage of* "cholo" *has varied widely in different times and places. In modern American usage, it most often applies to a low-income Mexican-American sub-culture and manner of dress.*

Wikipedia's explanation is confusing. I really don't understand it. I had to look up words such as *castas,* which means race or breed, and *criollo,* which means creole. Then I had to look up *creole,* of course. A Creole is a person of mixed ancestry. I was like, "What the hell?" *Chola* sounds more like an exotic dish.

I type *chola* into yourslang.com and it reads: *They usually have thin, arched, angry-looking tattooed-on or penciled-on eyebrows, bright red 'Marilyn Monroe lips,' nose piercings, huge hoop earings, Converse or Nikes, flannel shirts, lots of gold jewelry, crunchy gelled or moussed hair either slicked back, in a high pompadour, tied into a perfect ponytail, or left loose but highly styled, and they go out with* cholos.

A *chola* sounds like a goth or a pin-up girl.

Except for the red lip liner and the gold jewelry, I think Natalia has everything else. Especially the angry-looking part. She doesn't wear heavy makeup, but she does have those penciled-on eyebrows and ponytail, which is what I like the most—her thick, long, dark, shiny hair.

I close my eyes and there she is, knocking at my window. She's asking me to sneak out with her. We hop on her bike, a monster black-and-silver bike. I hold onto her waist. We are speeding all over East LA. All of a sudden we are at a beach. We climb off her bike, she pulls me towards her. We start kissing. We kiss passionately. We kiss as if there's nothing else to do. We kiss as if we want to become one.

We're about to kiss again when someone knocks at my door. It's Mom calling me.

"Baby, Tía Angela is here."

I don't want to open my eyes. I don't want Natalia to disappear. "I'm coming!" I yell. My hand is between my legs. I am rubbing, rubbing strong. I am coming, I am coming. When I'm done I decide to text Natalia.

Lady Maria here, thinking of you.

Translation: my face hurts because of the fucking ball you kicked at me.

I wait one, two, three minutes to see if she replies. Nothing. Then, my phone rings. A message from her:

You lucky.

I could have kicked your balls instead. (>-<)

This is the beginning of something, I know. I just know it.

CHAPTER FIVE
love. amor. amour.

AFTER PRACTICE I GO DIRECTLY TO MY ROOM. I don't say hi to my parents, to Aunt Angela, or even to Grandma. "Is everything okay, Mari?" Dad asks me. "No, of course not," I say. Mom asks what's wrong with me.

"I hate living in this barrio. I don't like school and I don't like the people at school." I go into my room and slam the fucking door.

"Give it some time, sweetie," Mom yells.

"It's only been two months," Tía Angela yells too.

"Two months is a LIFETIME!" I yell back.

"Let her be," I hear Dad saying.

There are way too many things around here

that I hate. First, I don't have friends like the twins or like Aimée. Let me rephrase that: *I have Rita, period.* Rita's the super-nerdy girl I met before classes actually started. On my first day she sort of showed me around, and I was grateful, but she gets on my nerves. She reminds me of the sweet, well-behaved girls at Immaculate who are always stressed out about grades, homework, practices, exams, grades, etc.

Second, the Spanish. Fucking Spanish. I can't handle it. I understand a little more, but I feel stupid all the time. "How come your last name is Herrera and you don't know Spanish at all?" my classmates ask. Fuck them and fuck Spanish.

Third, the soccer team. I really like being on it, but the girls, they don't seem to like me. It's like they don't trust me. You can't be on a team if you're not trusted, you only end up running and running without getting a chance to get near the ball. The only thing I've got so far is bruises and my coach's evil looks.

And last, but not least, Natalia. Natalia's driving me crazy. I know she likes me. If she didn't, why would she text me all the time, or wait for her friends to leave so that she can walk me home? If we run into each other at school I don't exist: she walks around me and I'm invisible. But when it's only her and me, you can almost feel the tension between us. She cares about me. I know she does.

Yesterday, for example, I took her skateboard and I fucking tripped. She was like, "Oh my god, are you okay?" She had the sweetest caring voice ever. I fucking scraped my knees and the palms of my hands. Natalia sat down on the sidewalk with me, held my hands, and cleaned them off. "Does it hurt?" She asked me. Her eyes fixed on mine. She wanted to kiss me, I could feel it.

Then she sorta snapped out of it and said, "Come on, stand up, *Lloroncita*. It's nothing. Let's get you washed up." I couldn't believe it.

"You are an asshole," I told her and went straight home. She texted me all afternoon but I didn't reply.

I didn't even glance her way during soccer practice today and I went straight home after we were done. I head straight for the shower.

"Mari, you almost done, sweetie?" Tía Angela asks me as she slightly opens the door to the bathroom.

"No, I'm letting the water run till it gets hot," I tell her. "Why?"

"We need to continue with the aloe vera treatment on that knee of yours." Tía is mortified about all the scars I get at soccer.

"I'll call you," I say.

I take off my clothes and look at myself. I am a mess. My life is a mess.

I get in the shower, it's still not hot yet. I let the cold water rinse away my dirt and these ugly feelings I carry.

Tía Angela yells, "Oh Mari, I just remembered. There's no hot water."

I get out of the shower, wrap myself in a towel, and stomp into my room. Tía Angela follows.

She sits next to me and opens the small tub of aloe vera.

"You okay?" she asks.

"I'm mad, so mad," I tell her. "I am mad at the freaking cold water. I am mad I can't understand shit in Spanish. I am mad because Rita never wants to do anything fun. I am mad at my soccer team. But mostly I am so, so mad at Natalia. Fucking Natalia." I curse without noticing it.

"Who?" Aunt Angela says and she stops spreading the gunk on my scraped knees.

"Never mind. It's just that I am so . . . "

"Mad, I get it," Aunt Angela says. "You know? Your mom used to be mad all the time when she was your age. Now tell me, who is this Natalia?"

"She's on my soccer team. She owns the skateboard that almost killed me," I say as I point to my knees. "She's Don Felipe's daughter. She works with him at the bakery."

"Oh," Tía Angela says, making a face. "*She* is

your friend?" Aunt Angela doesn't look so happy about this.

"Well, kinda. Why?"

"No, it's just—I don't understand how is it that you are friends."

"Why?" I ask again.

Tía Angela is now placing new Band-Aids on both my knees before answering.

"Well, how can I say this?"

"Just say it, Tía."

"You two are very, very different."

"Please don't tell me that it's because she was raised in a bakery and I was raised by nuns in a fancy school," I joke.

"No, no, it's not that."

"Oh, is it because she is *chola*-ish?"

My aunt bursts out laughing and says, "*Chola*-ish? What the hell is that?"

"Well, she isn't a *chola-chola*, you know. I've done my research and she's just a little bit *chola*." We both laugh. My anger fades away.

She caresses my head and says, "You remind me so much of myself when I was your age."

"What do you mean? What were you like?"

"Crazy, like you. Always making jokes, always laughing."

"And then, what happened?"

"Your uncle, that's what happened."

Tía Angela, just like mom, left home as soon as she could. The only difference is that my mom ran away to go to college in San Diego. Tía Angela did not dare run away. Instead, she got herself a boyfriend and got married very young. That was her only way out, marrying a man accepted by her parents.

I don't think there's anything wrong with marrying young, unless you marry an asshole. Like Tío Robert.

Tío Robert is like Dr. Jekyll and Mr. Hyde. In front of everyone he's the perfect man, but he is mean and rude and a total dick with Aunt Angela. For example, she isn't allowed to work or go to school and the only places she's allowed to go on her own are here to Grandma's or to the supermarket. He's super jealous of any man that even dares to look at her. Aunt Angela doesn't talk to men who don't belong to the family.

I don't know how she has put up with him all these years, but finally, she is leaving him. That's why she's been staying with us. I don't know all the details but it seems that she finally found the guts to tell him to fuck off. She's been here for a few days now and he hasn't tried to contact her or anyone else in the family. This makes me uneasy. Dad works for him in one of his shops. I'm sure Uncle Robert knows she is staying with us.

I hope Dad finds some other job soon.

"Do you wanna talk about it?" I ask, even though I already know her answer. She's looking at me, like she's trying to find herself, her old self, in me.

"Oh, no, no. We're talking about you, about you and your friend."

"Right. Tía, why don't you like that Natalia is my friend?"

"I didn't say that. I just said that you two are very different."

"But different is good, isn't it?"

"Sometimes."

"Aunt Angela, just spit it out."

"Okay, okay, I'll try. The thing is, baby." Tía Angela is definitely Mom's sister. She does the same thing every time. When she is going to say something that might be harsh or weird, she calls me *baby*. A few examples: "Baby, your sister is dying, you know?" or, "Baby, we have to move back to East LA." Tía Angela looks at my room, as if she were trying to find the best words.

"Come on, Tía, spit it out."

"Look Mari, I know one should not judge just by appearances, but your friend Natalia, she is very *butchy*, don't you think?" This is one of my mom's techniques as well: to minimize the impact of her words she adds a *y*.

"I don't understand."

"Well, don't you find her too *masculiney*?"

"As *masculiney* as any other girl who plays soccer."

"Come on, Mari, you know what I'm talking about."

"Even if she were too *masculiney* as you say, what's wrong with that?"

"Well, your mom certainly wouldn't like her."

"Grandma likes her."

"Oh, well, your grandma hired Vicky, didn't she? Even though Vicky is . . . "

"Vicky is what?"

"You know."

"No, I don't." I do know. But I want to hear her say it.

"Listen, just be careful, baby. She might misunderstand your friendship."

My blood's boiling. I know Aunt Angela has never been too open-minded herself, but is she homophobic, too?

Tía Angela looks at me before she stands up and walks out of my bedroom. I should let her go, I should, but instead, I say: "Or maybe you think that my friend Natalia is a lesbian and you're afraid that she misunderstands my friendship for love. But what if it's me who wants my friend to be more than a friend?"

Tía Angela comes back to where I am sitting. "I would say that you are confused. *Very* confused."

"What if I am not? What if I am in love with a girl?"

"Don't say those things!" Tía Angela yells, and then she slaps me. "Your mother has had enough in this past year, you can't do this to her, Maria." Maria, that's what she called me. There's no doubt now, I am different. I am not my old self. I stopped being Mari.

"Do this to her?" I bark. "This has nothing to do with her! Nothing!"

"Are you telling me you have feelings for that girl?"

"Just—just leave, Tía. I don't wanna talk about this anymore."

"Mari, are you in love with that, that *chola* girl?" she asks, her tone changed.

"Maybe I am. It's hard to explain."

Tía Angela sits back next to me. She grabs my hands and says, "Sweetie, it's better you forget about whatever it is that you *think* you feel for her before it turns into something ugly." She looks at me, she pats my back and stands up. "I should go and help start dinner. It's late."

"Wait, Tía, talk to me." But she's already gone.

I start getting dressed when I hear my phone. Text messages. From Natalia.

Are you still mad at me?

Are you like not talking to me . . . EVER?

I'm about to text her back, but I change my mind. I know what will happen: I will text back. She will make me laugh. We will start talking again, and then we'll be back to hanging out without anyone noticing until she, again, acts like an asshole.

Maria Maria Maria Mariaaaaa

I decide to ignore her text, but then she strikes back again:

Maria. Please. Talk to me.

I wanna type, *What you want?*, but before I do so, I get one more text from her:

I am sorry about the other day. I get this stupid when I'm into someone, I'm an ass when I like someone.

She likes me. She likes me! She likes me? I wanna jump. I wanna run to the bakery and kiss her. I start to type something, but she texts one more time:

Fine. You don't wanna talk to me I get it. It's cool, whatever.

Fucking Natalia. Fucking, fucking Natalia. She wants things her way.

* * *

"Mari, dinner is ready!" Grandma yells from the kitchen.

At dinner, only Mom does the talking. She shares

with us stories about her job. She's the only one who seems to have an actual life. She seems happy; she says this is the first time her work actually makes a difference. I look at Grandma's smile. She's proud of Mom. Dad smiles, but he doesn't look happy or proud. Aunt Angela shares Dad's sentiment, a smile that is just there to hide sadness. I know it because I'm doing the same, smiling as if everything in the world was just fine. But it isn't.

I wish Glo was here. Glo would understand— or at least try to understand—what we are all going through, what *I am* going through. Glo was the only one in the family who knew the truth about me.

It happened when I was in sixth grade and my sister was in eighth. That year, we were in the orchestra class together and a new girl walked in. Louise.

Louise was probably my first love, although I didn't know it. I didn't know that what I felt for her was something other than friendship. She was my sister's age. She joined our school later in the fall semester. Classes had already started and everyone was friends with someone already. She joined our band, and like Glo, she was a wonderful musician. She played the tuba and stood near me. I just couldn't keep my eyes off her.

One morning, as we were waiting for the school bus, Glo just went for it and asked me, "Do you like Louise?"

"Yeah, she's great. Why? You don't?"

"Well, yes, but you seem to like her more."

"More?"

"I've been watching you lately. Promise not to get mad?"

"Promise."

"Swear to tell the truth, the whole truth, and nothing but the truth . . . "

"So help me God."

"Do you have feelings for Louise?"

I started nodding before she could even finish

her sentence. "No wait, I know you do. What I mean is, do you feel attracted to her?"

"I don't understand."

"Do you feel attracted to her the same way that a girl feels attracted to a boy?"

"Wait, what?" Glo's words sounded strange and familiar at the same time. I thought about it for a minute or two: was I attracted to Louise? Did I like her the same way that a girl likes a boy or a boy likes a girl? I didn't say yes, but I didn't say no. Instead, I said, "I don't know. I just, I just like her."

"I know you do—you look at her all the time. You like her. You seriously like her."

"Nonsense. I like her just the way you like your friends. I've seen you, you drool when you see Monica."

"I don't drool when I see Monica. I drool when I see Monica's shoes." The bus arrived at that very moment. It was already packed with girls from school, so my sister simply added, "Let's talk about

122

it later. But don't worry, if you do have feelings for her, your secret's safe with me."

I did, I liked Louise. I liked her the way that gives you butterflies in your stomach. That night after dinner, Glo and I were watching TV. Our parents were out at some charity dinner. Glo asked me if I had thought about our conversation. I nodded.

"Wait, before you say anything I want you to know that I love you no matter what. You're my sister, and I know we sometimes argue over stupid things, but I love you, I love you bunches. And if it happens that you like Louise, that you do like girls, know this: it's okay."

"Please don't tell anyone. I think, I think you're right, I do have feelings for Louise. I like her, Glo. I can't stop looking at her. Today, after we talked, all I did was think about her and her beautiful green eyes and her long fingers playing the tuba."

"I knew it."

"Are Mom and Dad going to kill me?"

"They don't have to know. Maybe, this is just

something that happens to you with Louise, maybe it's just a phase."

But it wasn't. What's even worse, Louise didn't share those feelings. Louise had a boyfriend and he watched her play in the concerts at Immaculate.

Louise was the first girl I fantasized about when I took those long baths. Then Aimée came to the picture.

Glo was the only person in my life who knew about my true feelings. Now Glo is gone.

* * *

Dad brings me back to the present with this: "Mari, you okay? You've been too quiet."

"Yeah, yeah, I was just listening to Mom," I said as I drank the last bit of tamarindo juice from my glass.

"You better watch it, Mari, that tamarindo juice can become dangerous tonight or tomorrow at school," Grandma says.

"What do you mean?"

"Well, *tamarindo* has laxative properties, which means . . . " Mom started saying, but Grandma jokingly finished the explanation, "That you might be pooping and pooping the next couple of hours."

"Yuck, Grandma, I'm eating!" I yell.

"Well, it is the truth," Dad adds. "You better watch it or tomorrow instead of running to defend the ball you will be running to the restrooms."

"You have a game tomorrow?" Mom asks me.

"Yes, we're playing against Garfield."

"Wow, hey, how do you like this new team?" Mom asks.

"It's okay," I say.

"Have you made many friends?" Aunt Angela asks, and I notice a distinctive tone when she does.

"Yeah, some."

"Oh, I heard Don Felipe's daughter practices with you. How is she?" Grandma asks innocently.

"Okay, I guess. We don't talk all that much," I say.

"Why? Because of her *chola* friends?" Grandma asks me.

"Natalia? *Chola* friends? I am lost, what are we talking about?" Dad asks as he looks at both me and Grandma.

"I don't know if she is really a *chola*," I say.

"Well, she does dress like one," Tía Angela inserts.

"Oh, I forgot you are a *chola* expert, Auntie," I say. "Natalia isn't a *chola*. She just kinda dresses like one," I explain.

Vicky walks into the kitchen with Grandma's medicines. "Natalia *is* a *chola*. She is just a very young one, and because Don Felipe is so strict, she doesn't follow the whole *chola* code."

"How do you know, Vicky?" Grandma asks her.

"Because I've known her since she was a kid."

"You have?" I ask her.

"Oh my god, this *chola* issue is like one of those telenovelas your Mother watches, don't you think, Samuel?" Mom tells Dad.

Vicky ignores my mother's words and continues, "Yes, and that girl is trouble, believe me."

Aunt Angela looks at me like she is saying *I-told-you-so* with her eyes.

"Well, now I am dying to meet this Natalia," Mom says, "You say she plays with you, Mari?" Mom asks intrigued.

"Yes."

"Well, I guess we'll meet her tomorrow."

After dinner, I go to my room. I feel something. What is it? What is it? I lie on the carpet, my legs up on my bed. Arms spread from my sides. I close my eyes.

Loneliness, that's what it is. Loneliness.

I miss my sister, I miss Aimée.

To: aimeedelphy98@gmail.com

From: mari_herr@gmail.com

Subject: Get me out of here!!!!!!!!!

Oh Aimée, I wanna get the hell out of here. Things suck big time. I know I've never been too friendly, but here I have ONE, only ONE real friend. But my one real friend drives me crazy. Her name is Rita, and she's nothing but nice to me, but there's like only two things we talk about, the weather and school work. Rita is always stressed about her grades. She says, "Look Mari, the only way to leave this place is by getting a full scholarship into some college, and how do you do that?" I simply shrug, she answers her own question, "Well, I'll tell you how, Mari. The only way is by being the best of the best, Mari." She's the only person outside my family that calls me Mari, and I think that her overusing it has made me hate my name, seriously.

Rita wants me to volunteer with her on this com-mittee or that. She wants me to go along to any event the school organizes. "It's a good idea to be seen as someone who cares about the community. What do you think, Mari?" Can you believe it? Poor Rita, here I am talking shit about her while she's next to me writing a list of common phrases in Spanish to help me get by.

There's this other girl I hang out with sometimes, but she is way more complicated than Rita. I will tell you all about her some other time. Rita is about to give a short seminar on the use of the letter ñ.

Anyway, how are you?

xoxo,

M A R I A

p.s. What the hell is JTK? I see you use it on all your emails. Is it like xoxo?

CHAPTER SIX
better off

I WAS CONSIDERING QUITTING THE SOCCER TEAM BECAUSE: one, we suck; and two, I just don't seem to fit in. But today at the end of practice, the coach had a long talk with us.

She said that we were all great individual players, but we were an awful team. "Don't you wanna win?" she asked us. We do, we all want to win, of course. "It's time to change," she said.

So she is taking us on a weekend retreat. We all have to ask our parents to sign permission slips. I'm sure my parents will be happy to see me doing something else besides watching telenovelas with Vicky and Grandma.

After practice I overheard Natalia telling the coach that she might not make it to the retreat. "You see, I work on weekends," she said. Our coach reminded her that as both our goalie and our captain she *had* to go. Our coach even offered to call Natalia's dad. I don't see why he wouldn't let her go.

It's nine p.m. and by now Natalia is already out of work. I should text her and ask how it went with her dad. Who knows if she will reply, she has been ignoring my last couple of texts.

I hate myself. Why do I have to like the one girl who plays hard to get? I open my computer and I find a new email.

To: mari_herr@gmail.com
From: aimeedelphy98@gmail.com
Subject: RE: Get me out of here!!!!!!!!!

Mari,

Changes are hard, aren't they? I understand you. It was hard for me, too. As I told you, I'm in a new school. I told my parents, "Send me back to California or get me into a different school." I didn't want to go back to my old school, and to those merde, those shitty "friends." It is because of them and their bullying that I left France last year.

Oh, but enough about that. This new school was hard at first, but then something happened. SOMEONE happened. I met a girl. No, let me rephrase that: I met THE girl.

JTK,

A.

P.S. JTK means Je te kiffe, we use it a lot, it's a way of saying I like you. In English it feels different, it loses its beauty. I guess that we use it as you guys use the xoxo or I love you, or something. We also use JTA which means Je t'adore, which translates into I adore you. Just know, Mari, that when I say JTK I am sending you a big hug and lots of love.

So, Aimée met *the* girl. She is better off than me. I met *a* girl, a girl who makes my life both wonderful and miserable. I wonder if love between boys and girls is just as difficult as it is between girls and girls.

"Hey sweetie, how was school?" Mom says as she walks in my room.

"Fine, how are you? You look tired."

"We had this long meeting with the board. We need more funding and they didn't seem to get it, but at the end I think I made my point clear."

"You like your job, don't you?"

"I do. It's just, there's so much that could be done at the clinic if we had an actual budget. But enough about me, what are you up to?"

"Not much."

"How's school going?"

"Well, it's going. Oh, by the way, I need you to sign this for me," I say handing her the permission slip from my coach.

"What's this?"

"The coach wants to take us on a retreat."

"A retreat?"

"Yeah, we need to build our team spirit or something. Our team has great players, but together we seem to suck."

"Wow, someone seems excited to be playing soccer again," she says smiling. "I think moving here has been good after all. We're better off here, right?"

"Right."

"I just wish your dad would start feeling the same, too. He hasn't been able to find a new job since he left the furniture store."

"I know. It sucks," I say.

"He needs a job or a hobby before he turns to telenovelas just like your Grandma and Vicky." Mom smiles. She indeed looks happier. The change has been good to her.

My telephone rings. It's a text from Natalia.

"Okay, I'm gonna take a shower and then head

off to bed, baby," Mom says as she signs my paper. "So, when is this thing?"

"Next weekend," I tell her. Mom leaves my room and I open Natalia's text:

Believe it or not, mi Jefe said yes and signed my permission slip for the retreat. Are you going too?

Yes, Mom just signed mine.

Cool. Let's sit together on the bus.

Yes, let's.

I will bring some *conchitas* if you'll bring something to drink.

Sounds like a plan.

Wouldn't it be cool to share rooms too?

Cool? No, it would be more than cool, Natalia and me together. Now I'm really looking forward to this thing.

CHAPTER SEVEN
life changing

I CAN BARELY SLEEP. DAD DROPS ME OFF AT SCHOOL at five forty-five a.m. When I get inside the bus, Natalia is already there. She saved me a place. As soon as we get on the road, all the girls get their pillows out to sleep.

Not us. I brought a thermos with *café con leche* and she pulls out a brown bag with *pan dulce* from her bakery. We are the only ones awake, talking, eating, laughing. We ignore the girls around us who keep yelling at us to shut up.

When we get there, we are all shocked at how beautiful the place is—so different than anywhere in East LA. The coach points at the cabins where we'll be staying.

"Each one has two bunk beds," she says. "So all of you will be sharing a room. I hope you do actually get some sleep." She's right. Four girls in a room sounds more like a party.

There are eighteen girls on our team. In a second all of them start making small groups. Before we realize it, Natalia and I are left alone. We look at each other and smile. The coach goes, "Now, take a cabin and put your stuff inside, then come back and we'll get started."

Natalia and I are in the same cabin. It will be interesting. She's all cool and relaxed. She is two girls in one. Natalia is cool. She's fun. She listens to you, she really does. But when she is in her *chola* mode, she's just a pain in the ass. Today she is being herself and not Rat the character she plays when those two mean bitches, Drizella and Anastasia, are around.

This is day two, and I must admit, the whole

retreat has been life-changing so far. It's been fun. We've laughed so much, there's this new spirit around us: it will definitely help us boost our performance on the field. What's best is that we haven't even played soccer at all. The coach and her assistant have been organizing games, activities, and competitions to create trust, to learn about strategy and taking initiative.

Last night we were all so tired that we went to bed super early. But tonight, we are making a fire and we are going to roast s'mores and drink hot cocoa. Our coach is making us share personal anecdotes. Each one of us has to tell the rest of the team two stories. One, the happiest memory of our lives; two, the saddest memory. "Because we need to learn to appreciate both the good and the bad of our lives. It is what makes us who we are," she says.

I talk about the first time Glo and I flew on a plane on our own to a summer camp in Oregon. Everybody laughs when I tell them that we ended up hanging out with this old lady because we were scared to be alone. For my saddest memory I tell them about Glo's death. As I share details about her last days in the hospital Natalia's hand starts caressing my back. I didn't notice when she came to sit next to me. All of the girls who did not trust me, the same girls who would make fun at my lack of Spanish, offer sweet, warm words to me.

Now it's Natalia's turn. I don't think I have ever seen her like this. She is nervously rubbing her hands against her legs. Her two stories are shocking. I can't believe what I am hearing.

Natalia's best memory is also the beginning of her worst. It has to do with her brothers. Natalia's brothers always played on their own. "Male bonding, that's what they did all the time, and I was nothing to them. But this one time, they were missing a player for their soccer game. So they invited me. *Me!*"

"It was a whole day of fun and jokes and messing around," she said. The boys were older than her and played pretty rough. She was dirty and bruised by the end of the game. Her legs were all scraped up from sliding on the not-so-grassy field. "But I didn't cry. It felt good. I was happy to be part of the game, to be part of something," she tells us.

The problem came later, when she got home and her mother saw her all beat up. She was so angry and asked Natalia how she had gotten that way. "*Mi jefa*, she had always known I wasn't the girliest girl in the world. Only this time, this time she let me have it." Natalia's mom beat her up while yelling, "*Marimacha, marimacha*, that's what you are." I've heard this word, *Marimacha*. Vicky told me about it: it means "a macho woman." Like "butch" in English. Sounds way more insulting, though.

"She hated my guts because I wasn't the daughter she imagined," Natalia continues. "I had two options. Become what she wanted me to be or own who I am. I'm sure you know what I chose. I mean, it's clear I'm no lady. But my mom couldn't stand the sight of me."

The story does not end here. Natalia tells us her mother kicked her out. "It happened after I told her who I was, so I had move in with my old man."

We are all quiet around the fire, processing her words, putting together the pieces of the girl we know as Rat.

Then one stupid girl says, "Natalia, you can't be mad at your mother. She's probably just worried about you."

Natalia takes the last piece of her s'more and throws it in the fire. I hear her whispering a firm, "Fuck you," as she gets up and walks to the cabin. We all look at each other, clueless as to what to do. After a few minutes, the coach says, "Herrera, go with Gomez, see how she's doing."

I find her outside our cabin. She is sitting down on the porch.

"Hey, want some company?" I say. Natalia looks at me and shrugs. I sit next to her.

"How come you never talk 'bout your sister?" she asks.

"How come you never told me 'bout *your* mother?" I respond.

"You miss her, your sister?"

I nod, then ask, "How 'bout you? You miss your Mom?"

"Never," Natalia answers firmly.

"I can't imagine," I say without thinking.

"You can't imagine what?" she asks me, kinda upset.

"Never mind."

"No, tell me, you can't imagine what?"

"You living with a woman like that. Thank god you left."

"I left her, yes, but she didn't leave me. Her words are here all the time," Natalia says, pointing at her gut. "Every time I push people around, every time I punch someone's nose just because I want to, she is with me. I can't help it."

"Well," I started, regretting already what I was about to say, "Maybe that side of you isn't completely about your mom, you know?"

"What do you mean?"

"Well, those people you hang out with . . . How can I say it?" I try to sound nice.

"My *clica*? What about them, Maria?" Natalia snaps. She stands up now, her hands on her waist. Rat the *chola* is coming out. She's putting up her guard, like she does on the soccer field. "Tell me, what's wrong with *my* friends?"

I know I shouldn't be saying a thing, but I am Mari no more, I am Maria. "Friends? Those two are no one's friends. They're fucking bullies. Everyone at school hates them. They beat people up, like that poor freshman kid—they broke his glasses and took his money." I'm amazed at my own words.

I expect Natalia to give me the worst of the worst. I expect Rat to bark back at me, her fists on my face.

But Rat seems defeated. She sits back next to me and says, "I know, I know, believe me I know. But I can't walk away from them. I just can't. I owe them a lot. They're the only family I have," she says as she sits down again.

"Come on, Natalia, it can't be true. What about your dad?"

"Him? It's like I don't exist for him."

"Oh, that can't be true," I say.

Natalia looks at me and says, "To him I'm only an employee."

"Don't say that."

"It's the truth. I'm only here for the family business," Natalia confesses sadly.

This sucks. Natalia works so much with her dad. I put my hand on her shoulder and tell her, "You have me, Natalia. *Me.*"

Natalia looks at me. "I know," she whispers as she leans on my shoulder.

I feel confident, more confident than ever in my life, back when I was simply Mari. "I like you, Natalia. And I know you feel the same." Natalia tries to pull away, but I pull her back, I hold her tight.

"What are you doing, Mari?" she asks.

"Maria. My name is Maria," I say. My heart starts beating fast. My hands are sweating. My hands on her shoulders pull her closer to me. I start kissing her.

I kiss Natalia. Her whole body is now relaxed and eager for my embrace.

I loosen her ponytail and slowly run my fingers though her silky black hair. I sweep a lock of it behind her ear. I do it all without taking my lips off hers. We're alone. The murmuring from the other girls chatting around the fire are far away down the hill. As my hand moves to her cheek, Natalia pulls me closer to her face. She takes the big leap.

"You know I like you too. I told you I did, remember? I like you Maria. I think of you all the time." Before I know it, she's standing up, taking me by the hand. She walks me inside our cabin and starts kissing me again. Our lips, our tongues, our hands trying to figure out where to go, where to touch. My hands are on her thighs, her hands are on my back. The soft kiss quickly becomes more powerful with love.

"Herrera, Gomez, you okay?" the coach calls out. We push each other away. Natalia yells as she opens the door, "Yeah, yeah, everything is fine."

"Come back to the fire—you're missing all the boy gossip," the coach says.

Natalia and I join the rest of the girls. We walk next to each other, the backs of our hands touching. Before we arrive at the firepit, I squeeze her hand and whisper, "I want you." Natalia's eyes betray her shock. We sit on the same log. Close enough to feel each other's body heat. We exchange looks once in a while, smiling without smiling.

For the first time since we moved to LA I feel happy. Very happy.

That night, Natalia stayed in my bed. We didn't do anything besides kissing and cuddling. I had never slept so well in my life. Her sugary smell embraced me the whole night.

CHAPTER EIGHT
yes to the yeast

LIFE IS GETTING BETTER AND BETTER.

This is the best day ever, the best Friday of our lives. We won our first game. It was great. I had forgotten the feeling of victory. Even though it wasn't part of the regular season or anything, it was just a friendly scrimmage against Catalina High School, it feels like winning the World Cup. We had to celebrate—all the girls decided to meet up at Mario's Pizza Joint. My parents drove me there, but I convinced them not to pick me up. "I'll walk home with the rest of the girls," I said. I can't believe they said yes.

We're having a great time. We're eating tons of

pizza, talking about soccer, and laughing at each other's stories. It's almost eight p.m. and even though this is going great, all I can think about is Natalia. I want to be alone with her. I decide to text her:

Hey, what about splitting?

Splitting?

Yeah, let's go somewhere, you and me.

¿Escaparnos?

Yes, let's escape.

I want to be with Natalia, alone. It seems like she wants the same. She reads my mind. We keep talking about the game with the rest of the girls and then Natalia says, "Hey you guys, we're leaving. This *nerda* here needs to be home and I work tomorrow early." All of our teammates yell *No*'s and *Why?*'s, but we leave without arousing any suspicion.

"Where to?" Natalia asks me.

"I dunno, you are the tour guide tonight," I say smiling.

"Thought you had it all planned out, Maria."

"Nope, and I am open to suggestions." Natalia

looks at me, she looks at her watch and then says, "How about *un pancito*. You know, something sweet."

"Dessert always sounds good to me."

Natalia and I start talking about the game and our teammates. As we continue to walk, she tells me a bit more about her family. I try to ask her about her *chola* friends. Again, she doesn't say much, "One day, I promise you, one day I will tell you all about them and why I owe them so much. Just not tonight. Tonight is for us."

"Tonight is for us, I like it." I look around. We're alone in the street, so I grab Natalia's hand, and squeeze it for a second. I'm sealing a pact. Before I let her go I say, "Natalia?"

"Yes?"

"Have you, have you *dated* another girl before?"

Natalia freezes for a second and let's go of my hand. "Oh, are we *dating*?" she laughs. "Because I wasn't informed."

"No, no. I don't . . . it's not . . . I was

wondering . . . Just tell me, have you dated a *girl* before?" I can feel my face blushing.

"Before *you*?"

"Come on, you know what I mean."

"Yeah, I guess I have."

"You guess? What does that even mean?"

"It's hard to explain. Let's not talk about it now."

"Okay." We keep walking in silence.

Suddenly she says, "How 'bout you Maria?"

"What about me?"

"You know, have you dated a girl before?"

"I, I sorta, kinda did once."

"Sorta, kinda? How's that?"

"Well, I liked her, she liked me. We made out a couple of times, but she just wanted to be friends."

"Oh, a girl-scout."

"A girl-scout?"

"Yeah, a girl that is just exploring her possibilities. Not a real *jota*."

"She wasn't a scout. She knew she liked girls, but

she was an exchange student, so she wanted to keep things, how can I say it?"

"Friendly."

"Yes."

"Were you *enamorada*?"

That's a good question: had I been in love with Aimée? I used to think I was, but what I felt for her is very different from what I feel for Natalia.

"I don't know."

"Are you a girl-scout, Maria? Are you, you know, experimenting with me?"

"I'm not a girl-scout, but I do wanna experiment with you. Experiment a lot," I say as I grab her hand. If as Mari I was a scared mouse, as Maria I'm a badass flirt.

Natalia looks around and says, "It's better if no one sees us holding hands around here, people talk." She notices my disappointment, and says, "But we're here and no one will disturb us, you'll see." We are standing outside Natalia's bakery. The place where it all started.

"Here?" I ask her while she gets her keys and opens the back door of the bakery. Natalia invites me in without saying a word. She closes the door and then, "Yes, Maria, our *dating* starts here." She then grabs me by the waist and holds me close to her.

I cannot help but smile and say, "So we *are* dating then?"

"Do you want to?"

I don't answer. I close my eyes and give Natalia a kiss. Her hand moves under my shirt and up my back. I do the same. We kiss and moan and kiss and moan.

"Come here." Natalia pulls me by the hand. We walk into the kitchen. There are bags of flour and sugar and boxes all over a table. Natalia starts moving them.

I see a bag of yeast and ask, "I have never understood how yeast works."

"What do you mean?" she asks without looking at me.

"Yeast is like a fungus, isn't it?"

"Yeah, so?"

"So how come you use a fungus to make bread, isn't that bad?"

"You can be so smart and so dumb," Natalia says as she turns to me. She takes me by my waist and lifts me onto the table. She's so strong.

"Fungi are not all bad. This fungus, yeast, converts the sugars in the dough into carbon dioxide."

"Huh?"

"It helps the bread to rise. Yeast makes it fluffy and soft and delicious." Natalia looks at me. Her index finger draws a trail on my face and says, "Like your lips. Your fluffy delicious lips. You understand now? Yeast is a good girl."

"Yes, and yes to the yeast. Yeast rules," I say, "Now let me see if your lips are yeast-friendly too." Natalia is standing in front of me. I pull her close and embrace her with both my arms and legs. We make out again. I feel my heart pounding in my chest.

"You smell like sugar," I whisper in her ear.

"Hello? We are in a bakery. Of course it smells like sugar," she replies.

"No, *you* smell like sugar. You always smell like sugar. *Always.*"

"When I'm all stinky and sweaty after soccer practice, I don't."

"Then you smell like brown sugar."

Natalia smiles and we kiss again. I'm going for it. This is my chance to do what I've been fantasizing about. I unbutton Natalia's shirt little by little. She is wearing a sports bra. I touch her breasts over the fabric, then slowly pull it up.

"I wonder if you taste like sugar too?" I say before kissing then licking her nipples. "Yeah, you taste like sugar." Her eyes are fixed on me. I can't believe I'm doing this.

Natalia stops me for a second. "Maria, you trying to get to second base?"

"No, I play soccer, remember?" I joke.

She smiles and takes her turn lifting my shirt and touching my breasts.

"You taste like sea salt, like Santa Barbara beach sea salt," she says after tasting both my nipples.

It's almost eleven p.m. when Natalia says we have to go. I want to stay. "My parents won't say anything. Come on, let's stay a little longer."

"I can't. Dad doesn't like me being late. Besides, I really do have to work tomorrow."

"But it's Saturday," I say.

"Maria, I work every day, every single day."

"You must have a fat savings account."

"No, I don't."

"Why? How much do you make a day?"

"How much do *I* make? Nothing, zero, *nada*."

"What? Your dad doesn't pay you?"

"Nope."

"But, that's not fair. You work *a lot*."

"Well, it's the family business, after all."

"Yeah, but . . . You are family and you are working in it."

"And?"

"Well, you should get paid. I mean, your Dad is making money, isn't he? This is everyone's favorite bakery."

"Because we know how to make things, baby," Natalia says and gives me one last kiss before walking me out of the kitchen.

Making out is all we've been doing ever since. I sneak out to meet Natalia outside her bakery to be alone, to be together. It's easy, since my room is more like an annex with its own door—I can come and go without anyone noticing. Just in case, I always leave a bunch of pillows under my covers pretending to be me.

At school it's becoming a bit hard to keep things normal, but we've managed it. We just *Hey* to each other, and that's it. Sometimes we exchange a few words, just the necessary stuff during soccer practice.

She still eats lunch with Drizella and Anastasia. I normally eat with Rita who keeps asking me if I am dating someone or if I'm secretly in love.

"Why?" I asked her.

"Because you look different," Rita says. "You look happier."

"Well, I don't know what to say."

"Just say it. Tell me I'm right."

I think about it for a second. Rita has been very nice to me. I feel I can trust her. "There *is* someone," I say.

"I knew it! Who is he?"

I look around, making sure no one hears us. I lean over to Rita and go, "It's a *she*, actually."

Rita jumps from her seat and says, "Oh my god! This is way better than I expected. Tell me, tell me all about it!"

I tell Rita about *the* girl, I just don't tell her who this girl is no matter how much Rita begs. I tell her that the girl in question and I met yesterday at my place. I take Rita out of the cafeteria. We sit down outside on a bench.

"My plan was to fool around in my own bed with her, but she wasn't comfortable. She jumped at every little sound. She was too nervous someone might hear us."

"Of course. I would be freaking out," Rita adds.

"But no one could have found us, Rita. I told her that my Dad is always in his room watching TV, that my Mom comes back from work too tired and passes out immediately after dinner, and that Grandma, Grandma sleeps like a baby."

"Still, I'm sure she didn't feel safe. So, nothing happened?"

"Nothing."

"Is she your first?" Rita asks.

"Well . . . "

"Jesus, girl you are full of secrets."

I tell Rita all about Aimée too. It's comforting to have someone to talk to about all this.

To: aimeedelphy98@gmail.com

From: mari_herr@gmail.com

Subject: . . . .

I have news to share. I have ALSO met THE girl. But I won't say a word until you tell me about yours. I won't say a word about her until you do. No, Aimée, no I won't tell you that her name is Natalia and that she is fantastic. I won't tell you she plays soccer with me. I won't tell you how tonight we had sex, yes sex, on a table in her bakery. Oh yes, I also won't tell you that she and her father own a bakery, the greatest in the barrio.

So don't ask. I won't say a word. I won't tell you how wonderful it was to be entwined with her. I won't tell you about her soft, sugary skin. I won't. So, don't ask. If you want the whole story, then tell me about THE girl, YOUR girl.

JTK! XOXO

M.

CHAPTER NINE
angel angela

My parents had to go to Santa Barbara to sign the final papers for the sale of our house, so I am on my own for today's soccer game. Tía Angela offered to come and be my cheerleader, but I told her there was no need, things are still weird between us because she doesn't like Natalia.

Natalia's father never comes to the games. She's on her own, too, so it's been decided that after the game we're going to give it another try in my room. It's a perfect plan because on Saturdays, Vicky isn't with us, and Tía Angela is taking Grandma to play Bingo.

Before the game starts, I see Rita in the bleachers. I wave at her, then I see Natalia's *chola* friends, Drizella and Anastasia. I had never seen them before at any of our games or practices. They aren't alone. There's this other girl with them. A super-butchy, super-tall *chola* girl who looks older than any of us. The three of them sit in the bleachers close to the field.

Seeing them there takes Natalia by surprise. I can tell by her face.

We start off strong. We score a goal during the first minutes of the game, but as time goes by, Natalia starts showing signs of distraction, anxiety. She isn't playing as well as she normally does. She isn't focused.

Our coach uses halftime to give us a hard time. "We have been doing so well since the retreat, and now, now we are sinking, girls," she states. She turns to Natalia and asks her what's wrong. We are all waiting for her to answer.

Natalia says nothing.

"Focus, Gomez—just focus," our coach says.

Natalia simply says, "Will do."

Before we go back to the field, I ask her if she's fine. Natalia nods and leaves me on the bench. She is anything but fine. As she walks to the goal, she keeps looking at the bleachers where her friends are sitting. We can all hear them yelling, "Rat, look who's here. You gotta fucking win."

"What's with those girls?" I hear one of our players ask. Someone else answers, "La Flaca is back, that's what's happening."

Who the hell is this La Flaca? And why is Natalia so, so off?

We are losing, two to one. Garfield has just scored a second goal. I can't believe it. I was just sent back to the bench again, one of those Garfield girls hurt my knee. I'm okay, but I ain't going back to the field, that's for sure. My replacement is working hard, but what's the use of defenders if the goalie is elsewhere?

Our goalie is not giving it her all. Natalia isn't her usual self.

I can hear both the cheering from the Garfield people and the *Boo*'s and *Fuck-you*'s from Natalia's friends. Now that girl, La Flaca, starts yelling, "*Ándale*, baby, *ándale*. Just finish this game so we can all just go." She doesn't call her Rat, she doesn't call her Natalia. Baby, that's what she says. Baby.

The game is almost over. I thought we had zero chance to win when one of our girls scores a second goal. We are tied, two to two. If we can only score one more.

The referee blows the whistle on one of our girls. A penalty, a fucking penalty. The whole game is now in Natalia's hands.

"Come on, Rat, just fucking catch it," her friends yell. "You show them. You show them who is *my* girl."

The ball escapes Natalia's hands. A goal is scored. The game is over! Natalia throws herself flat on the field like a little girl throwing a tantrum. The rest of the team, we do what is left to do. We shake hands with Garfield's players. Not Natalia. Natalia stays away from of us.

I see her there, now sitting down, holding her knees. I decide to go to her, to cheer her up—this isn't the end of the world after all. It's just a game. I sit down next to her, and I am trying to figure out what to tell her when her friends start yelling, "Who the hell is that?"

"Oh, that's Whitey. *La Blanquita*, from Santa Barbara."

I pay no attention to what they say. "Natalia, it's okay. Don't feel bad, it's not your fault."

"Fault? Who said anything about fault?" Natalia has disappeared and Rat is here right next to me.

"I didn't mean it that way, I just don't want you to feel bad."

"Just leave, girl, go away."

Girl, she called me *girl*. As if I was just one of her teammates. I place my hand on her arm and say, "I'm not leaving you here. Come on, let's take a shower and go to my place."

She shakes my hand off and says, "What the fuck, Maria? Just go." Her friends start yelling, "Hey Rat, is that *Blanquita* giving you a hard time?"

I am losing my temper. These girls have nothing but a bad vibe. "This is none of your business," I yell at them.

"Shut the fuck up, Maria," Rat says, then she whispers. "You don't mess with them."

"Like I'm afraid. They're just words," I tell Natalia.

"Look, just go home. I'll text you later."

"What's wrong? I thought we had a plan."

"Goddamn it, Maria, leave! Just leave." Natalia stands up and leaves me there.

Everyone has left the field. People are walking off the bleachers too. I stay a little longer there, next to the goalposts. Then I hear someone calling my name. "Mari, you okay?" I thought it was Rita, but no, it's Aunt Angela and Grandma. They came to the game.

"Yeah, I'm okay."

"Let's go," they both say. "Let's get something to eat, *mija*," Grandma adds.

I stand up and walk off the field, "Okay, let me just take these off. I stink."

I go all the way to the locker room. A few of the girls are still there, getting ready to leave. I don't see Natalia.

I go directly to the showers. The water starts running when I hear Natalia's voice say, "What are y'all doing here?"

"We wanted to give you a *sorpresa*, Rat."

I recognize Drizzela and Anastasia's voices. Then I hear that girl, La Flaca, asking, "Baby, you missed me?"

"When did you get out?"

Out? Out from where? Had this La Flaca been in a madhouse or what?

"*Ayer.*"

"Yesterday, really?"

"Yeah," Anastasia adds, "They let her out for good behavior."

Good behavior? What the hell are they talking about? I hurry up, turn off the water, and get out of the shower wrapped in my towel. I don't dare to walk out. I hide behind the lockers so I can hear them.

"Well, that's good, right?" Rat says. "How come you didn't call me or anything?"

"I did. I called you like a million fucking times, *mija*. I called you from my bro's cell phone, but nada. You never answered."

Last night Natalia and I were together, and yes, I remember her phone ringing. She didn't recognize the number, so she didn't answer. Plus, we were kinda busy.

"Oh. I . . . I guess I missed it or something. *Perdón*."

Sorry? Natalia saying she was sorry? That was new, not even when she was in her kindest moments would she apologize.

"You betta be sorry, cause I just spent two months in juvie because of you," La Flaca said.

"I told you not to. I told you not to take the blame for what happened," Rat said, "Didn't I?"

What's all this about? I get my clothes and dress in a hurry. The talking turns into yelling.

"What the fuck has gotten into you Rat?"

"She's a *blanquita* now, that's what's happening."

"*¿De qué hablas?* I don't know what you mean. Why am I a *blanquita?*"

"You and *la blanquita*—making eyes at each other, hanging out. We've seen you around with her."

"*Cállate*, you don't know what you're saying."

"Have you forgotten 'bout me then, Rat? *Ya te olvidaste de mí, de tu Flaca?*"

"You broke up with me. *¿Te acuerdas?* You said it was over. That's why I stole your brother's shit."

"*Cállate*, don't you think I know that? *Pinche* Rat. You just don't get it, do you?" Then I hear some punching or hitting.

I decide to come out. "Natalia, what's going on?"

"*Mira, la blanquita está aquí.*"

"She ain't a whitey and she ain't mine," Rat says, "Just let her go. Leave, Maria. This is none of your business."

"I'm not going anywhere. I'm not leaving you here with these three."

"*Mírala qué macha*," La Flaca says. "She's a *macha*, this whitey."

"Don't call me *macha*." I am actually more *macha* than ever now. I don't know what has gotten into me. I hate Drizella and Anastasia, our school bullies, and now I also hate La Flaca.

Rat goes, "Listen, Flaca, I don't even know what you guys are doin' here. You broke up with me, and if you don't remember, *es tu problema*. I'm sorry you took the blame for me, for stealing those drugs, *pero ese es tu problema*, too. I didn't ask you to do it."

"Shut the fuck up, pinche Rat," Drizella yells pulling Natalia by the arm.

"*Déjame en paz!*" Natalia yells. "I'm off, I don't care 'bout you all. Don't care about that chick either." She points at me, and to my surprise, to everyone's surprise, she leaves. Natalia simply walks away, leaving me here with these girls.

In my mind there are two thoughts: one, they

will let me go—of course they will—her whole deal is with Natalia, not with me; and, two, why did Natalia leave—why did she leave me here?

"What's this one's name again?" La Flaca asks.

"Maria, I think," Anastasia says.

"Yup," Drizella states. "She is in my math class, and believe me she is even worse than I am."

"She new in the barrio, then?" La Flaca asks.

"Yeah, she's a rich girl from San Francisco."

"Santa Barbara," I say.

"Oh, from *Sannna Barbrra*," Drizella says, making fun of me.

I shrug and start walking away.

"Hey, where you going, girl. You running away from us?" La Flaca says.

"She's not running away," says Drizella.

"She wants to go after Rat," says Anastasia.

"Doesn't she know that Rat is taken already?" La Flaca asks.

"Rat *ya tiene novia*. Look, *she* is Rat's girlfriend, not you," says Drizella, pointing at La Flaca.

"She isn't my girlfriend," I say.

"Then why are you always with her?"

"Yeah, like her puppy dog, *su cachorrita*."

"I am not."

"Yes, you are, we've seen you," says Drizella pulling me by my shirt.

I take her hand off me and push her away.

"Don't they teach manners in *Sannna Barbrra*?" says Anastasia.

La Flaca comes closer then grabs me by the shoulders. "Natalia *es mía*, only mine. You betta watch it, *blanquita*."

"It doesn't seem that way," I say. "Didn't she just walk away *from you*?"

I don't even know why I said that—the situation was already pretty bad. My words just made it all worse. Everything happens so fast. First La Flaca slaps me and grabs me by the hair and starts pulling me down. I hear Drizella yelling, "*Dale, dale duro,* Flaca," and all I can feel is La Flaca's fists on my stomach, my face. She is everywhere. She is punching me hard, too hard. Now Anastasia is also beating the shit out of me. Three against one.

I see fists, I feel fists everywhere. They get my left eye and now I can't see a thing. I can't do anything. I give up trying to fight back. Then I hear Aunt Angela's voice scream: "Let her go! What the hell are you doing?"

The beating suddenly stops. My aunt pushes through Drizella, Anastasia, and La Flaca and kneels down to me.

"Sweetie, are you okay?" Aunt Angela yells. "I'm calling the police!" I had never heard Tía Angela like this. I can't see clearly, both my eyes are swollen, a halo of light surrounds her. She is an angel—Angel Angela who came to my rescue.

"Vámonos, vámonos," La Flaca says, they all leave in a second. A minute later I hear a voice, "This way, hurry." It's Natalia.

"What's going on here?" It's the coach, the coach is here, too. "Oh my god, Herrera, are you okay?" But it hurts too much to say anything, I close my eyes.

CHAPTER TEN
take it or leave it

I HAVEN'T SEEN NATALIA SINCE THE DAY THOSE GIRLS beat the shit out of me. Vicky tells me that she comes and rings the bell. But Mom and Aunt Angela won't let her come in. They blame her for what happened. Vicky says that Natalia stays outside and sits on the sidewalk. Today she spent three hours waiting outside.

"She was just there, looking at your windows," said Vicky, who came to check on me late in the afternoon. "*Mija*, I told you Natalia was trouble, but I felt bad for her."

"Why don't you like her?" I ask Vicky. "You of all people should understand her."

"What do you mean, Mari?"

"Vicky, I'm gonna tell you a secret, but promise you won't tell my parents. Promise you won't tell anyone."

"What is it, Mari? *Me pones nerviosa.* Tell me what is it?"

"Natalia and I, we . . . "

"You are friends, I know. You are friends even though I told you to be careful with her."

"It's not that."

"Mari, what's going on?"

"Natalia and I, we're more than friends. We like each other." Vicky is trying to understand my words. She looks at me in awe. "Vicky, we are in love." Vicky stands up from my bed and walks around in my room. She stands next to my big window, the one that looks at the street. She doesn't move. She doesn't say a word, but I can see the words flying through her mind.

Finally, she says, "Are you serious, Mari? Is this why you were asking me what *jota* meant?"

"Yes, I'm serious. I am not confused if that's what you're thinking. I like her. I like girls. I always have." I am tired of lying on my back and try to sit up, but everything hurts, my ribs, my stomach, my arms. "I'm sorry I didn't tell you about this the other day. You opened up to me and I didn't. Vicky, I'm sorry. I truly am."

Vicky comes to my side, sitting next to my bed. She takes my hand and says, "Oh Mari, there's nothing to be sorry about. Don't apologize. I understand. I understand it all now." Vicky caresses my hand, tears fall from her eyes. She looks at me and a sad, beautiful smile shows on her face.

"Why are you sad, Vicky?"

"Look at you, Mari. Look at what those girls did to you! This is all Natalia's fault. She left you on your own with those girls."

"No, Vicky. She tried to help me. She went to get help. She is great."

"That's where you are mistaken, Mari. I know

her. Everyone in the barrio knows about her. She's no *blanca palomita*."

"*Blanca palomita*? What does that mean, Vicky?"

"She is not as innocent as you think."

"I know she seems that way, but she has had a hard life. All because of her mother. Her mother was abusive and mean, she would call her names because of the way Natalia is."

Vicky looked shocked. "Martha would never abuse her. She would never place a hand on one of her kids! She is a wonderful woman. You got it all wrong, Mari. Believe me, I know what I am talking about."

"Natalia's mother kicked her out."

"No, that's a lie. Martha tried so hard to be a good mother for her, but Natalia's always been trouble. She ended up in juvie like a year ago. That's why she's now with her father. And Felipe's only worry is to make money."

"Why would Natalia lie to me?"

"I don't know. And I don't know exactly why

these girls attacked you, but I know it's got something to do with Natalia. That's why she keeps coming over. She feels guilty. *Me da pena,* I feel for her."

"You know Mom turned my phone off and put it away? I can't text her or call her."

"It's better this way for now."

"No, Vicky you gotta help me. Help Natalia sneak in so we can talk."

"*¿Estás loca?* No way, Mari. I'll get in trouble. We both will."

"Please, Vicky, please. I need to see her. I need to talk to her. I need to understand why she lied. I need to know what exactly her deal is with that girl, La Flaca."

"Oh, I know what her deal is with La Flaca, believe me. That one is also *puro problema.*"

"Vicky, you know so much about Natalia, why?"

Vicky lets go of my hand and stands up again. She stands right in front of me. I see her face red and pinched. "Because, because we all live in the same barrio."

"You seem to know more than anyone else, though."

"I have known her family since forever," Vicky states, but there's something fishy about her words. I go, "How? Are they your friends, Vicky?"

Vicky paces across my room then finally sits back next to me and says, "Because Martha and I, because Natalia's mom and I, we are together. I mean, sorta together. You understand?"

"*What?*"

"We met when we were both very young. We were in love, but her parents wouldn't allow us to be friends. She ended up marrying Felipe who is a macho just like Roberto, your uncle. Martha left him, and well, now we're trying to make it work."

"I can't believe it, Vicky. Does Natalia know any of this?"

"Of course she doesn't. Martha never dared to talk about . . . about *us*."

I can't believe it. I can't believe all these secrets and stories behind Natalia's family. Why did she lie to me?

"Vicky," I say. "You gotta help me see her."

"No, Mari. That's not wise."

"Vicky, Natalia is a mess. She gets in trouble every time things get rough for her. You know she stole drugs or something from La Flaca's brother?"

"No, that was La Flaca herself."

"No, it was Natalia, she did it because La Flaca broke up with her. And now, if we can't meet, if she thinks I'm mad at her, who knows . . . who knows what she'll do. Vicky, please, I beg you."

"No, Mari. It's too risky."

"Do it for me, please."

"No, Mari. I can't."

I'm about to lose hope. "Vicky, don't do it for me, at least do it for Martha. I'm sure she doesn't want her daughter to end up as fucked up as those *chola* girls."

Vicky looks at me and sighs.

Mom comes and gives me my pain medicines before she and Dad go to bed. "You look better," she says. "You wouldn't believe two days ago you were all messed up."

I smile and say, "I feel better too, I'm sure I'll be able to go back to school soon."

Mom looks at me, all serious, and says, "Listen, baby." I'm alert to her sugar-coating code word. "Your father and I've been thinking. We're going to find a different school for you."

"I don't need a new school. I like César Chávez. I like my team. Don't make me change, please don't."

"Baby . . ."

Here it comes again.

"I know you like your team, but it's been a hard adjustment. I guess we didn't think things through when we decided to move here."

"I'm happy at my school now. This thing . . . this thing that happened . . . it has nothing to do with my school. Please Mom, I don't wanna go to a different school."

"Listen, we'll talk about this again in a few days. You must rest. Want me to turn off the light?"

"No, Vicky said she would come to say good-night," I say, lying to my mother. Vicky is coming, yes, but she is actually helping me sneak Natalia into my room.

"Okay, night-night."

"Hey, Mom, where's Aunt Angela? She hasn't come to see me all day."

"Oh. Well, she is back home."

"What?"

"Yes, she's back with your uncle."

"She what? Are you serious? Why?"

"Well, he apologized to her."

"And you let her go? Mom, you know he's crazy."

"Mari, it is not our place to judge your aunt's decisions. Now, rest."

This is really fucked up. I get beat up and my aunt decides to go back with her ogre husband.

I take my aunt off my mind and try to sit up straight. My whole body still hurts, but I feel happy. I will see Natalia after these two long days. I reach for my mirror and look at myself. "I look like shit," I say.

Vicky comes to my room and says in a hushed voice, "It's all set. Natalia just texted me. She's on her way. She will text me again once she's outside."

"Thank you, Vicky. Did she say anything else?"

"Nothing."

"Have you talked about this with her mom?"

"No need. She already knew. Everyone knows those *chola* girls beat you up."

Vicky's phone rings. She's got a text.

"She is already here. That was fast! I don't even know if your parents are in bed yet."

"Don't worry about them. Please go get her."

Vicky walks out, closing my door behind her.

I feel butterflies up and down in my stomach. I've missed Natalia. I haven't even given too much thought to the fact that she lied to me about her family and her friends. I just want her to be here with me.

* * *

Natalia walks in. She is a mess.

"What happened to you?" I ask her, "Are you okay? Is that a black eye?"

Natalia is staring at me. "Oh my god, Mari, what have they done to you? Look at you. Are you okay?" Natalia comes and kneels down next to my bed. "Jesus, I am very sorry for all this."

"It's okay. I'm okay. It hurts less now. But how about you, what happened?" I try to reach to her face to touch her black eye and then notice that her lips are also swollen.

"Those bitches took it out on me, of course."

"*Cabronas*," I say.

"Ah, you curse in Spanish and all now?" Natalia says laughing.

I missed her laughter. I missed her. I ask her to

come and sit on the bed next to me. She does and kisses my forehead and apologizes to me one more time.

"Natalia, we need to talk. You and me," I tell her.

"I know, I know. See, Mari, I never told you about La Flaca because everything was over between us."

"No, Natalia. I don't want to talk about La Flaca. I mean, that's not all I wanna talk about with you."

Natalia lays her head on my shoulder and our fingers intertwine. "Watcha wanna talk about then?"

"Your mother."

"What about her?"

"Why did you lie about her. Why did you lie to me?"

"What do you mean?" she asks.

"Your mother she wasn't abusive. She never kicked you out. Your mother she loves you, Natalia."

"Who told you this? Oh, of course. It was Vicky, right? Fucking Vicky told you all this." Natalia stands up and paces by my bed. "Maybe I lied.

Maybe my mother didn't abuse me or she didn't kick me out of her house, not directly at least, but she did kick me out of her life. When she realized I was a *marimacha* she gave me a hard time. She was impossible. She said I would only suffer. A hypocrite, that's what my mother is. Did Vicky tell you that she and my mom are *marimachas* too?"

"I thought you didn't know. Listen Natalia, you don't understand."

"No, *you* are the one who doesn't understand, Maria. I tried to talk to her, but she wouldn't accept it. Perhaps she didn't beat the shit out of me as I said, but she did, in a way."

"She was only trying to protect you, Natalia."

"No, she was lying to all of us, me and my brothers."

"Natalia, it's not that simple. You gotta give her a chance, but most importantly, you gotta stop lying."

"Lying?"

"Yes, you don't have to lie to me. You don't have to do stupid shit just to prove yourself."

"I don't do stupid shit."

"You don't? What about stealing drugs from that chick's brother. How about getting *her* in juvie?"

"You don't even know what happened."

"Come on, Natalia, I know everything. I know how things happened. I know you guys were together, then she broke up with you. I know you stole that stuff and in the end it was she who took the blame. She probably did it to protect you. She probably did it because she felt bad about what had happened between you two."

"Oh, so now you are on La Flaca's side?"

"No, of course not. I hate her fucking guts."

Natalia wanted to smile, but she wouldn't. "Then, what the fuck is your problem, girl? Did you want me to come here just to tell me I am a fucking liar?"

"Don't call me *girl*. I am Maria, you know it. Maria. And I didn't ask you to come just so I could call you names. I wanted us to talk, so you could understand that there was no need to lie, no need to do stupid shit, no need to live with your dad when you could be way better off with your mom."

"I'm just fine living with my dad."

"No, you aren't. He's taking advantage of you. You told me yourself. He's so nice and kind on the outside—to the other people, to the clients. But with you, with you he is an ass."

"What?"

"You heard me, he's an ass. He makes you work too hard, and right now, there should be only two things on your mind."

"What, you and you?"

"No, you idiot, school and soccer."

"Shut up, you don't know what you're talking about."

"When was the last time he went to one of our games? When was the last time he bought you cleats?"

"Shut up, Maria, we aren't all fucking fancy like you."

"It's not that I'm fancy. It's that I am living with

people who *actually* care about me, unlike your dad. That's the truth, Natalia." I don't realize I am yelling now.

Vicky, who's been guarding the door for us, opens it, and asks, "Is everything okay?"

Natalia looks at her, then looks at me, and says, "Fuck you then, Maria. Fuck you both." These are Natalia's last words before she walks out.

"What was all that about?" Vicky asked me, her mouth hanging open.

I broke down and cried. "I lost Natalia. I lost her for good."

CHAPTER ELEVEN
the perfect fish

To: mari_herr@gmail.com

From: aimeedelphy98@gmail.com

Subject: Conneries

Dear Mari,

I haven't heard from you in a while, so I take it things are getting serious between you and THE girl. My THE girl? Well, she is gone.

Love sucks. Life sucks, doesn't it? Sometimes life is not fair, and there's nothing we can do about it. Claudine, that's THE girl's name, well Claudine broke up with me. Yes, as you read it.

But first let me tell you that I came out to my

parents because of her. I lost my parents' love because of her. They despise me, they despise that I am the way I am, a *lesbienne*. And then, Claudine stabbed me in the back. She broke up with me. She told me she couldn't do it anymore. She told me she was confused. She told me she didn't want people talking about us. She told me she didn't want to talk to her parents about (and let me quote) "Whatever this is." Can you believe her?

Connerie, bullshit, pure bullshit.

Please, write soon.

Aimée

To: aimeedelphy98@gmail.com
From: mari_herr@gmail.com
Subject: RE Conneries

Aimée,

I'm reading your sad letter. I'm sorry. I don't even know what to tell you. You're right: Love sucks, life sucks, it all sucks. I'm right there with you. We are partners in the broken-hearted district.

My story is a little bit different, but details don't matter. What matters is that I feel like shit, and I look like shit. Some girls attacked me. Yes, I was attacked. I was in bed for what seemed like an eternity. Now my parents want to send me to a different school.

To make things worse, my Aunt Angela is back with her husband. I don't know if I ever told you about her. She is Mom's younger sister, and she married this horrible *macho* man who treats her like shit. She had found the guts to leave him, but now she's back with him. Who understands relationships, really?

The only good thing that happened is that I finally decided to tell Rita that Natalia was my girl. She's been very supportive. She's now like the only friend I have.

I can't believe you came out. I can't believe your parents' reaction. I had considered talking to mine, you know, when things were going well in the *love district.* But now I don't know. I don't see the point of doing it. Really? There's no point in coming out.

To: mari_herr@gmail.com
From: aimeedelphy98@gmail.com
Subject: RE RE: Conneries

Of course there's a point in coming out!!! I don't regret coming out. Maybe the mistake was to open up BECAUSE I had someone in my life. I should have done it just because, you know? I should have done it just for me, to be honest about myself, with myself, for myself.

Mari, if the thought has been on your mind, just follow your instinct. Do it, Mari, do it, just do it. I won't lie. It's gonna be hard. You are going to feel they are disgusted. You are going to feel they despise you. But my sister, my dear sister, says I must be patient. She says parents love their kids and, at some point, they come around. Who knows? Maybe she is right.

Maybe your parents will be different than mine. They've been through SO MUCH already, I'm sure that little by little they will get it. They will accept you. But if this doesn't happen Mari, if they don't understand and accept you for who you are, fuck them! Yes, FUCK THEM.

This is your life, period. If Natalia doesn't come around, fuck her too, yes FUCK HER TOO. *"Un de perdu, dix de retrouvés,"* my grandma used to say. This means: one lost, ten found . . . I think it is like that phrase you guys use, "There are other fish in the sea."

You will see, Mari, when least expected, we— you and me—will find the right girls for us, maybe even ten! We will find *the* perfect fish, Mari.

You were right, you said in one of your letters that we are not alone because we have each other, and yes, we do, we do have each other. We always will.

JTK, JTK, JJJJTTTTKKK

CHAPTER TWELVE
new in the barrio, again

So it's happening again: we are moving, we are changing our lives. After months and months of not working, after months and months of filling out applications, going to interviews, and getting rejections, Dad got a job.

It's not just any job in a furniture store, it's a big-time job. He says he's back on track. He's so excited that he looks like a kid who has just gotten a gold star for good behavior or something. Mom, Mom is not so happy. I'm not happy either. This job, this fucking job, is in San Diego. So now we all have to leave our lives again and move on.

Mom is having yet another argument with Dad

about this whole thing. "I am proud of you, believe me. But I don't want to move. I like my job. I like this clinic a lot. I think I am actually doing something that matters for the community," she says.

"Honey, we all need to make sacrifices. It's not like we are going to let this chance go just because you like your job. Besides I will be making plenty of money. There will be no need for you to work," Dad says.

We are all in the kitchen finishing the *arroz con leche* that Grandma prepared. It is my favorite dessert. It was Glo's favorite too.

"But I like to work. I have always worked," Mom states. She has the face of a kid whose toy is being taken away. She isn't eating her arroz con leche, she is just moving it around with her spoon.

"I know you do, honey, but understand my position," Dad says as he keeps eating. "This is my chance, this is *our* chance to make it big again."

I try to just listen, mind my own business. But I can't.

"I know that I don't get to decide this, but can I just say what I think?" Dad stops eating. Mom turns to me.

"I don't wanna make it big. I don't wanna move. *We* shouldn't move. We are fine here."

"What? This is coming from the same person who, not so long ago, hated this place *to death*?" Dad says.

"I never said *that*."

Mom and Dad look at each other, both of them nod, and say, "Yes, you did." In this they agree— great.

"Well, people change. And I changed my mind. I like it here. I'm happy here. I'm all better here."

"Are you? I still remember your Aunt Angela's phone call less than a month ago telling us you got beaten up by some barrio girls."

"That was just me being in the wrong place at the wrong time. Besides, I can't just leave in the middle of the school year. The last time we moved, we waited until the end of the school year."

Dad looks at me and Mom looks at Dad as if agreeing with what I've just said. If the school year doesn't convince him, I can always use the Grandma card: we can't just leave her alone again. I wouldn't be lying. I do feel we shouldn't just leave her. But before I get to say anything my grandma goes, "Listen, Samuel. *Yo nunca me meto.* God knows I never ever meddle in your life." She's pouring the hot milk into her crystal cup. The milk turns brown as it touches the instant coffee.

"But," Dad says as he turns to look at her.

Grandma walks to the table, pulls out a chair and sits down right next to me. "But you don't have to go, not all of you; at least not right away."

"What do you mean?" Dad asks.

"You know, I think I understand where your mother is going, honey," Mom says. Is that a smile on her face?

Grandma continues, "Listen, accept this job if that is really what you want. You go on and find yourself a small apartment in San Diego. See how it goes. See how you feel."

"You can even start looking for a place for all of us, with no hurry . . . " Mom adds. I'm starting to understand where they are taking all this.

"We girls stay here with Grandma. Mom won't have to suddenly quit her job and I can at least finish out the school year."

Dad is seated at the end of the table. All of us are on his left, Mom, me, and then Grandma. We are all waiting for him to say something, anything. He just looks at us, then takes a look at his arroz con leche as if trying to find answers in it.

"I don't know. Family is supposed to stay together in good and bad."

"Ay, Dad, don't be old fashioned. Just give it some thought."

"Yes, Samuel, we will be fine here. You can come every weekend," Grandma adds.

"Besides I wouldn't like to leave my sister just now."

"But she is back with Robert," Dad states.

"Yes, but that won't last, *mijo*. And who knows what that idiot is capable of?" Grandma adds. She is on fire now. She really never meddles with Dad's decisions, but this time, she is going for it. "Robert *es un cabrón*, you know that. It's best that she feels our backup. You know, she is a daughter to me as much as Gloria is."

"Come on, Dad. Maybe once you're there you won't even like it," I add.

"But I was already thinking we could now afford a private school, just like Immaculate Heart of Mary."

"Oh no, no way. You're not sending me back to Catholic school. No sir. If we do move to San Diego I wanna be in a school just like César Chávez."

"Where girls beat girls, you mean?" Mom adds.

"Oh my god, for the eleventh time, what happened had nothing to do with school. Besides, whose side are you on, anyway? San Diego or East LA?"

Mom smiles, and giggles a little.

But my dad isn't laughing. "I don't know. I do

understand what you're saying, but it doesn't feel right to leave you all."

"Ay Samuel, *por dios*, we will be just fine," Grandma states.

Dad looks at each one of us before he says to Grandma, "What about you, Mom? Would you move in with us once I have everything all set?"

"And leave my house, *dejar mi barrio?* No way, Jose. *Ni loca.* I can come down and visit you, but this is my home."

"*Viejita necia.* Stubborn. You are such a stubborn woman, Mama," Dad says.

"I mean, I don't know. Maybe at some point I will decide to leave all this, but now, I still have things going on here. We all do. I still have some clients, special clients. And Gloria has her job and she is happy with it, and Mari . . . well, Mari still has some figuring out to do here."

"Figuring out? What figuring out does Mari have to do?" Dad asks me.

"I dunno, school?"

"No, *mija*, your team and your friend Natalia. You still have to figure that out." Grandma has just thrown a bomb here, what does she mean by that? What does she know?

"Natalia, the girl who got Mari in trouble?" says Mom.

"Natalia, Don Felipe's daughter?" says Dad.

"Natalia who is a very special friend for Mari. Mari can't leave without straightening things out with her."

Mom and Dad look at me. I can almost trace the question marks on their faces. What's all this that Grandma is saying? Where is it all coming from?

Dad breaks the silence and says, "Well, I need, we all need to think this whole thing through. Let's not jump into any decisions." Says the one who wanted us all to move tomorrow. He stands up and leaves the kitchen. Mom goes after him, which leaves only Grandma and me in the kitchen.

"So, *mija*, now that they're gone. How are things going with Natalia?

"What do you mean, Grandma?" I say without looking at her.

"*No te hagas la tonta*," she tells me—*don't you play the fool now*. "I know everything—I mean, almost everything—except why you guys fought."

"Everything? What's everything, Grandma?"

"*Pues que se gustan.*"

My face feels hot. *You girls like each other*, she said. "How do you know?"

"Ay Maria. I might get confused easily and all, but I know when two people drool for each other. You guys started drooling for each other when you met."

"What?"

"*Ay, me vas a decir que no.*"

"No, no, I won't deny it."

"Well, then tell me the whole story. I've been very polite and gave you your space, but believe me I've even been tempted to ask Vicky all about it." Grandma takes the bowl with *arroz con leche* that my mom left on the table and starts eating it. "Spit it all out. Come on, tell your *abuelita*."

Tears are rolling from my eyes. I can't believe she knew. I can't believe she's always known and has never said a thing and hasn't told my parents. She doesn't even look mad about it.

"Ay, *hermosa*, you're crying. *Dios mío*."

"I am not *hermosa*, Grandma. That was Glo. I am *preciosa*, remember?"

"Yes, yes, of course I remember. I'm sorry. I am getting old. *Mi preciosa*, tell me what is going on between you and Don Felipe's daughter?

I tell Grandma the whole story and she makes the same faces she makes when she is watching one of her telenovelas. Only now she isn't falling asleep. She's wide awake.

I tell her how after that night that Vicky and I sneaked her in, I haven't seen her. I tell her how Natalia quit the team, and then how when I finally saw her in school, she had no eyebrows, just a thin black line as if drawn with a sharpie.

"So she turned more *chola* than ever?" Grandma asks me.

"I guess so."

"And what about *esa*, La Flaca? She in school with you guys, too?"

"No. Rita says that she's probably being cautious because she doesn't wanna go back to juvie."

"Oh, so Rita knows about you and Natalia?"

"Yes."

"So only Rita and Vicky know about Natalia?"

"No, the twins also know, you remember they visited, don't you?"

"Oh, they know too?"

"Yes."

"Anyone else?"

"No. Well, yes. Aimée, my friend from France, she knows it all too."

"So you are like, how do you guys say it? Out of the closet."

"Kinda, I guess."

"Mmmhh."

"You mad, Grandma?"

"Well, of course I am. It seems like everybody else knew *but* me."

"My parents don't know."

"Are you planning to tell them?"

"I don't know. It's hard. I don't know how they'll take it."

"I understand, but tell me, is this serious?"

"What do you mean?"

"Do you like just girls, or are you biosexual?"

"*Biosexual?* Ha, ha," I can't help laughing. "No Grandma, the word is not *biosexual*, it's *bisexual* and no, I am not bisexual. I don't like boys *at all*. *Biosexual* . . . where did you get that from?"

"Television, *mija*."

"Right."

"Well, if you are—ay, I don't like the word—but if you are *lesbiana*, then I think at some point you have to talk to them. I don't mean that you *have to* tell them, but it's only fair that you share this with them, don't you think?"

"I guess you're right."

"Of course I am, I am your grandma, aren't I?"

"Yes."

"Did Vicky tell you how she came out, you know, with her family?"

"No."

"Very interesting story. Make sure you ask her about it before you talk to your parents."

"Okay."

"Did she tell you that she and Natalia's mom . . . you know?"

"Oh, Grandma you're so funny. Yes, she told me."

"Call me crazy, but I think that is what happens when men beat their women."

"What happens?" I ask her intrigued.

"Well, they leave them and find themselves a woman, a caring woman. Like Vicky. Believe me, I hope that one of these days your Aunt Angela leaves that *cabrón*, and finds herself someone as caring as

Vicky. I wonder if she has friends, you know, single friends?"

"Grandma, you're crazy! That is not why women prefer women. It has nothing to do with men. I can't explain. But it doesn't work like that."

"Yeah, Vicky also says I am wrong."

"Hey, Grandma, how come you never got married?"

"Well, single mothers have it hard, you know?"

"Mhh."

"And I guess I never found the right man."

"Right."

"Or the right woman!" Grandma adds laughing. We both laugh.

I have never felt so close to her. I understand now why Glo was so into her. I miss my sister. I wish she hadn't died, but I don't know—if it hadn't been for Glo's death maybe I would have never realized what a wonderful woman Grandma is.

"Come on," I tell her. "It's almost time for your telenovela. Let's go watch it."

"No," Grandma says as she stands up. She walks to the kitchen cabinets and opens her money drawer. "Let's go get us some conchitas and empanadas," Grandma says, stuffing a few dollars into her pocket.

As we walk together, I take a look at everything in the barrio. I would never have thought that I would like it this much, so much that I really don't want to leave it. Not just yet. Who knows? Maybe we will be able to convince Dad to let us stay a little longer. Maybe he'll end up hating San Diego and we won't have to move. And maybe, maybe, Natalia will get tired of being Rat and we'll work things out. Maybe, just maybe.

I hear a skateboard approaching from behind us, the scent of sugar surrounds us too. It's like the first day. It's like I am new in the barrio. Again.